THE MISTLETOE WISH

BINDARRA CREEK CHRISTMAS ROMANCE

SUZANNE GILCHRIST

MALLEE STAR ENTERPRISES

THE MISTLETOE

WISH

Bindarra Creek Christmas Romance

By

SUZANNE GILCHRIST

Apocalyptic/Dystopian:

Paying the Forfeit

Storm of Fire

Don't Look Back (Warders of Earth)

CONTEMPORARY SWEET

Bindarra Creek Makeover (Bindarra Creek Romance)

Cotton Field Dreams (Mindalby Outback Romance)

CONTEMPORARY ROMANTIC SUSPENSE

Endangered Heart

Scent of the Jaguar (Deadly Forces series)

FANTASY/ANCIENT WORLDS EROTIC ROMANCE

Bound by Love

Bound by Lies

THE MISTLETOE WISH

Cover Design by: Patti Roberts from Paradox Book Designs

First published in 2022.
Mallee Star Enterprises 2022

Written in Australian English.

Author Website: www.segilchrist.com

For my daughter. Always.

CHAPTER 1

Sara had dreamt about him last night, or at least someone who looked eerily similar to the man seated on the opposite side of the room. Surely it couldn't be him? No, that would be too crazy a coincidence. And besides, that one meeting had been a fleeting, less than one hour, experience. But it was odd how he had occasionally popped up in her thoughts; especially during those dark days when her life had imploded.

She kept her eyes resolutely fastened on the magazine she held in her hands. She was determined not to sneak another peek at the only other occupant in the solicitor's waiting room. Her back stiff with the odd tension hanging in the air, her vision blurred, so intense was her concentration. Neither she, nor the mystery man, had spoken since they'd been invited to take a seat and the receptionist had disappeared out the door.

The silence remained unbroken, the minutes ticking away on the antique clock which reposed on the mantle above the bricked-up fireplace. She was aware of his steady gaze and the tiny furrow between his brows as if he too harboured a curiosity towards her.

Outside the old building, sunlight broke through the heavy clouds that loomed grey and sullen over the small country town of Bindarra Creek. The thin beams streamed through the narrow, un-curtained window and in the air, golden dust mites swirled like drunken dancers. A faint rumble of thunder sounded in the distance. Despite being the first day of summer, the weather was cool although humid – unusual for this time of year – and the air conditioning was downright frosty.

Dressed in a thin cotton blouse, a navy skirt and wearing the only pair of sandals she possessed, Sara shivered then tossed the magazine onto the chair. It was useless attempting to divert her attention with a celebrity couple's matrimonial woes. Not when her mind teemed with so many unanswered questions – the forefront of which was – why was she here?

And the second, and the one that loomed larger, – who *was* that man? No name sprang to mind and yet she couldn't shake the sensation that she *had* met him previously. That he really was the guy who kept recurring in her dreams.

She snuck another glance, and her tummy rolled over as she found his cappuccino-coloured eyes fixed on her. Relaxed in his chair, yet he gave the impression that at any moment he could easily spring into action if needed.

She tore her gaze away and dug her short nails into the palms of her hands. What was it about him that kept drawing her attention? Shoulders wide enough to carry any burden? Or was it the steadiness of his gaze; as if he was someone who would accept people for exactly who they were. As if he was someone who would always stand by your side.

Sara glared at the inoffensive carpet. What rubbish. She had learned the hard way the only person she could truly depend on when the chips were down, was herself.

A movement flickered in the shadows beneath the coffee table.

Something furry skittered across her toes.

Emitting a shriek bound to arouse the dead, Sara leapt to her feet then, an instant later, somehow found herself standing on her chair. Heart in her throat, choking off another scream, she danced about, shaking first one foot in the air and then the other.

If there was one creature in the world that she was mortally terrified of; it was mice. A remnant of her poverty-stricken childhood that she'd never managed to conquer.

"Steady on. It's okay. Your ferocious dragon is long gone." The man's calm tones cut through the frantic pulsing in her ears. His voice rang with an authority that reassured; made her feel as if there was nothing he couldn't conquer.

Blinking, Sara ruthlessly buried the little whisper inside telling her here was a man she could trust.

There was no such thing.

He stood directly in front of her holding out a hand. No doubt intending to assist her off the chair. The faint lines at the corners of his lushly, lashed eyes deepened and his lips twitched but at least he had the decency not to laugh.

Heat scorched her cheeks. What a silly sight she must present.

Sara lifted her chin. Almost blindly she brushed his hand aside, took a step.

Her sandal slipped over the glossy magazine and … whoosh … she was air borne. Warm arms encircled her, catching her just in the nick of time. She let out a relieved breath only for her lungs to seize as reality dawned.

She lay half-hanging over the top of his head while his face … *OMG!* his face was buried between her breasts.

Talk about having a bad day!

An unwanted heat licked through her veins as she froze; mortified and confused by the fire igniting her blood into flames. This wasn't like her. She didn't do instant attractions. She certainly never waffled over what to do next.

"What is going on in here?" came an artic voice from the direction of the doorway.

Mumbling apologies, Sara wrenched herself free and landed on the thin carpet a good two metres away. She busied herself tugging at her clothes and soothing her tangled hair while the man muttered something about vermin in the building. She would *definitely* not think about how good it had felt to be held. By someone. By anyone. And how for one long unfathomable moment she'd wanted to sink into his embrace and shut out the world.

More shaken than she cared to admit, she almost blindly turned aside to pick up her handbag. She performed a quick check to ensure the zipper was secure thereby meaning nothing creepy or furry had scampered inside. Then she hurried after the other two as they trooped down a short hallway and into another room which was equally as dim as the one they had just left.

A man sat behind the huge mahogany desk, with a large window behind him. At first he appeared simply as an outline. By the time Sara had taken one of the two vacant seats, her eyes had adjusted and her equilibrium was restored. Yet a blazing question remained – why was the stranger here? She smiled at the local solicitor, Ty Devereaux.

Ty greeted her then turned to the silent man sitting next to her. "Darim Cooper, I presume?"

"Indeed." The man, Darim, leaned over and shook the solicitor's extended hand.

His name meant nothing to Sara. She must have

been mistaken when she'd thought she'd met him before today.

"This is most unusual." Excitement along with curiosity flared in Ty Devereaux's eyes as he flipped through a bundle of loose printed pages on his desk. "Before we start, procedures must be followed. Could you both please present me with your driver's license along with your passport if you have one or your birth certificate and Medicare card."

A few minutes passed while he perused their ID's and ticked boxes on one of the pieces of paper. After handing back their documents, he offered them a folder each. "Now allow me to inform you why you are here and then you can read the information provided."

Pausing, he took a sip of water before folding his hands on top of his desk. "Thanks to the generosity of a certain benefactor, you are now the joint owners of a property which consists of twenty-five acres of land encompassing a house, one windmill and two dams."

His statement fell into a pool of silence that seemed to last forever.

Eventually, Darim Cooper drew in a sharp breath but didn't respond. His chair creaked as he shifted his weight jarring Sara out of her shock. She actually wondered if perhaps she was asleep, dreaming.

Surely, she had misheard. Surely, her greatest wish had not just been handed to her on a silver platter. "I'm sorry, Mr. Deveraux, but would you mind repeating what you just said?" The words came out in a rush, almost tumbling together.

"Of course." A smile creased his face.

After he finished, Sara didn't feel as if she was any the wiser. "I don't understand." She shot a glance at the silent man beside her who shook his head, as if indicating he also was at a loss. "Are you certain you haven't made a mistake? I have no relatives in this country. I don't even know if I have anyone in the world that could be related to me. Both my parents came from a South Korean orphanage. And I've certainly done nothing to warrant such a gift, or a reward."

Quite the opposite in fact. The shame that never left her night or day, gnawed away in the depths of her soul. She made no move to rifle through the folder, instead she placed it onto the desk. Beating back her tormenting memories, she twisted her hands together where they lay hidden in her lap.

"I'm also confused and know of no one who would do such a thing." Darim tapped a finger on the papers he held as if emphasising a point. Although what that could possibly be, Sara had no idea.

Ignoring the man seated beside her, she fixed her attention on the solicitor, not wanting to miss one nuance of expression. "I'm certain you know more than what you are saying."

Ty Deveraux inclined his head slowly. "That is correct, however I am limited by client confidentiality as to what I can reveal, in particular the benefactor's identity. Basically, the bequest was initiated from the assistance you both gave a stranded gentleman approximately seven years back."

Sara shuddered and ducked her head. Seven years ago. A low point in her life that she had no wish to recall in any detail whatsoever. Her heart banged painfully against her ribs as she fought the flutter of panic beginning to hammer in her mind. Her muscles tensed. If the solicitor was about to mention her past, she'd be packed and gone before nightfall.

"Of course!" exclaimed Darim. "I remember now. I thought I had seen you before … Miss … er …"

Sara turned to look at him as Ty interjected helpfully. "Sara Pyeon."

Darim continued. "It was ten forty-five oh hundred and very cold, when I noticed a stationery car with its bonnet up on the road ahead." Here he paused and a pulse ticked to life beside his left temple as if not all his memories were pleasant. "We were coming back from a family holiday visiting the natural springs in Moree and my wife was keen to reach Singleton before dinner that night. As I pulled over, another car coming in the opposite direction also stopped. That was you, I believe." His sharp gaze drilled into hers.

So he *was* that guy! But more to the point, she'd been mistaken; this appointment had nothing to do with her past sins. Relief was as intoxicating as the mulled home-made organic wine made by a pair of elderly local sisters. Sara willed her hands to stop shaking and rushed into speech as details of that chance meeting flashed into her mind. "I was heading to Bindarra Creek."

There was no need to divulge the purpose of what had been her first visit to the small town. "An elderly gentleman had suffered a puncture and when he'd attempted to retrieve the spare tyre from the boot, he'd fallen over. I think he had knocked his head on something because he seemed a bit dazed. Plus, there was blood on his face." She paused.

A faint smile appeared on Darim's face and his rich, brown eyes warmed with laughter.

Try as she might, Sara couldn't prevent the blush that swept up her neck when she recalled what had happened next. Determined to prove she was in control of her life, of herself, hell anything would do, she'd marched to the boot and hefted the tyre out despite Darim's declaration to leave it for him. But the tyre had been heavier than she'd expected. She had staggered backwards, and the tyre had slipped out of her hands. The next instant, it was rolling merrily down the highway with Darim chasing after it – much to the delight of the little girl watching from the backseat of his car.

It had taken another hour before they were able to wave the old man on his way. He'd asked for their names, Sara now remembered, although he had made no mention of his own. "So, the man we helped has given me a house as a way of saying thank you?"

When spoken out loud, the idea hardly seemed feasible. There was no such thing as a free ride. There had to be a catch. Something the bloke would want in return. Or maybe this was all some elaborate hoax?

Darim must have been thinking along the same lines, as a heavy frown chased away any lingering amusement. He pushed the folder across the desk towards the solicitor. "I don't believe in fairy godmothers or fathers."

"It's all perfectly legal and above board. I assure you there is no mistake," Deveraux said in an affronted voice. "There are however certain conditions that must be met and adhered to before the property is transferred into your joint names."

"Joint?" Sara said.

Almost in unison, Darim queried, "Conditions?"

"Exactly." Ty began to read from the uppermost document. "Stipulation number one: both parties must reside in the house for no less than twelve months from the date of signing the agreement. Stipulation number two: neither party can sell, will or donate their share until that period has ended. Stipulation number three: if either party stays away from the property for more than twenty-four hours at one time, unless both parties are together, than they forfeit their share to the other party. An emergency obviously will not count, however said emergency must be authorised by the executor. Work related issues also come under this heading. Stipulation number four: no additions or alterations to the size of the main house is to be carried out during this period, apart from any repairs to ensure the dwelling is up to livable standards. Stipulation number five: any repairs or maintenance required must be run past the executor for approval and authorisation for the works to proceed."

He looked over first at Sara and then Darim. "There are more conditions, but they are minor ones. Now I do have another appointment soon, so let's get the ball rolling. I'm sure you are both eager to inspect your new home. I need your signatures here, here, and here. Don't worry, I will get my assistant to make a copy of the agreement for each of you."

Head whirling, Sara hovered the pen above the line marked with her name. It was if she was being tempted or tested, rather like Eve with the apple. Try as she might, however, she couldn't resist this once-in-a-lifetime opportunity. This could be her only chance of achieving her dream - owning a little land where she could run a home business making rugs and wall-hangings from llama fibre. The pen slipped from her clammy fingers. Flushing a little as she felt the men's eyes resting on her, her hand shaking, she snatched up the pen and signed.

As soon as Darim had scribbled out his signature, Ty plucked out two key rings from a document box and handed them one each. The solicitor stood, indicating the meeting was over. He offered a couple of his business cards. "Read through the information I have given you. If you have any further questions, don't hesitate to contact me. Remember, as executor I must approve any changes you wish to make to the property and will conduct regular inspections to ensure that you both adhere to the conditions."

A few minutes later, Sara found herself standing on the footpath outside the solicitor's office. She stared at the keys in her hand as the first few drops of rain landed on her hair and another roll of thunder crashed across the cloud-filled sky.

The man who she now had to live with for the next twelve months joined her, tossed his keys into the air and caught them.

His grin warmed rich chocolate eyes such a stunning contrast to his light sandy-brown hair, revealing a dimple in one deeply tanned cheek. "Race you there?"

"I have something I need to do first." Like gather her few possessions together then head for her three-hour shift as security guard at the hospital. She couldn't renege on the work – she needed the money.

Darim nodded. "See you later then." He marched off, slapping the folder against his muscular thigh and leaving her looking after him.

Her heartbeat quickened as a vision of a sprawling country house set amidst rolling green paddocks rose in her mind. It was if someone had waved a magic wand and she'd been granted her wish; albeit with strings attached.

Twelve months she had to share the house with that bloke.

But how hard could it be?

They'd have their own rooms, possibly their own bathroom. She could ensure she'd rarely cross paths with him. Maybe they'd have to meet every so often to discuss repairs, or fencing, or whatnot but nothing more. She probably wouldn't even notice when he was in the house! And she knew how to make herself invisible to others when necessary. Another lesson she'd learned the hard way.

Slipping the keyring into her handbag, she walked to her car. Her gaze snagged on the festive decorations adorning the front window of Penny Lane Bookshop, in particular the fresh sprig of green and white mistletoe.

She finally allowed herself a smile. Anticipation sizzled through her veins like the finest champagne. This was her chance for a future that would shine as brightly as the star on top of a Christmas tree.

All she had to do was find a way to get rid of Darim Cooper – then all her dreams would truly come true.

CHAPTER 2

R ain lashed the windscreen as Darim sent his Land Rover jostling and lurching down the muddy track that wound through dense bushland. The wipers put up a valiant effort but lost the battle against the deluge falling from the dark sky. Trees bent under the power of the wind and every so often branches scraped against the side of his barely six-week-old car. His stomach growled, reminding him it had been several hours since his last meal. It had taken him longer than he had hoped to finish off the paperwork on his desk and send in his request for leave. By the time he cleared his application with his commander and packed his gear, night had fallen early thanks to the storm rumbling overhead.

He leaned forward and squinted through the glass as his headlights caught something small and shiny. But it was nothing more than a discarded drink can. He swung the steering wheel a hard right, just avoiding in the nick of time the tree stump in the middle of the dirt track. Cursing under his breath, he wrestled the vehicle through a stubby bush then back onto the slippery pot-holed road.

Road! What a joke. Judging by the thick under-growth the previous owner had done nothing in the way of clearing the land. Nor any work on maintaining the track that led to the house for that matter either. He should have realised the moment he drove over the cattlegrid and had his first sight of the tangled and broken fences he'd have his work cut out.

But no way could he pass up the opportunity of making a home for his daughter. Celeste had made it more than clear the last time they had spoken that if he wanted shared custody then he had to provide some-thing more permanent than various Army base quar-ters. It was time he took his role as a father seriously or it would be too late to forge any kind of relationship with his only child. Of course, he could have purchased a house elsewhere but the lure of having family close by had been the clincher. His daughter, Skye would have instant friends with her cousins living in town. So, it was a done deal for him to settle in Bindarra Creek. Problem was there were few and far between properties for sale in his price range.

And now he had been granted this gift. Almost like a stupendous early Christmas present.

Leaning forward, he rubbed at the condensation fogging the glass hoping to spot the gleam of lights. Still nothing. Where on earth was the house? He was fairly certain he hadn't taken a wrong turn. In fact, there had been no other tracks leading off the one he was currently on.

The onslaught eased to a drizzle just as a clearing came into view. Lightning forked through the dark clouds. Thunder cracked. Darim rolled the Land Rover to a halt and stared at what he could see of the building lit up by his car's headlights. With a snap, he shut his open mouth.

The solicitor had termed it a house.

Darim stared at what could only be called a shack.

For the next twelve months he had to live in that … that place before he gained ownership. Well, his and Sara Pyeon's until he bought her out. The heady sense of satisfaction that had filled him upon hearing the news of his unexpected windfall vanished. Doubts reared their niggling heads and he'd wished he'd taken the time to read the agreement thoroughly before he'd signed. But the solicitor had been keen to get them out of his office, citing another appointment. Now he wondered whether Deveraux's actions had been deliberate in order to fend off any further questions. That didn't make sense, however, as the solicitor had invited them to contact him at any time. Maybe he had wanted to fend off any unwanted questions about the identity of their benefactor.

Darim switched off the engine and sat there turning over possibilities and probable future problems in his mind. There was no point in denying that the building in front of him was no bigger than a miner's cottage. If there was more than one bedroom, he'd eat his Army slouch hat for breakfast.

Evading his new house mate would be impossible. The memory of soft womanhood pressed against him and how his lungs seemed to drink in the musky, fruity scent of Sara's perfume washed over him like a great ocean wave. His gut tensed and he cursed as his blood headed south. That bloody moment when he stepped forward to help and she'd fallen on top of him. How he wished that had never happened. It had ignited thoughts – and needs – he didn't want. He had to keep his mind focused on the prize – a home for his daughter.

A home that did not include another woman.

A pale golden light appeared as Sara opened the door and stood on the threshold with a hurricane or oil lamp in her hand. Her expression, or what he could see of it, was stony and unsmiling as she stared at his car. Those fascinating almond shaped eyes of hers were inscrutable; an uneasy reminder that ever since earlier that day, she'd appeared far too often in his thoughts.

His fingers drummed on the steering wheel. He could just make out the dark shape of another vehicle parked beside the house. No other lights gleamed through the lone window which meant no electricity, which in turn probably meant no running water. Just what exactly had he gotten himself into? Only time would tell. He shrugged into his oilskin and clapped his Army hat onto his head. Bending low, he left the shelter of his car and splashed across the yard. When he reached the narrow front porch, he stopped. "Please tell me, it looks better inside."

"Come in and see for yourself." She moved back a pace, holding the timber door open with one hand. The lamp shifted with her movement, sending a wavering beam over the interior.

Darim removed his hat and heavy coat, taking a moment to shake the water off before entering. His muscles bunched tight and a hard knot formed in the pit of his belly.

Not even *one* bedroom!

He could be in trouble.

The *'house'* consisted of one cramped room, no more than five metres long by two metres wide. On his left was a concrete sink with one tap, a single cupboard next to it on the right and an old-fashioned coal or wood burning stove signifying the sum total of the kitchen area. In the corner directly opposite the *'kitchen'* was a camp bed which had a single mattress on top and there was a chest of drawers placed along the wall. Both looked relatively new which indicated Sara had brought them with her. Folded blankets and a doona along with a bulging duffle bag reposed on the bed. Obviously, she had claimed that space as her own.

Carving out another *'bedroom'* for himself let alone a room for his daughter was simply not feasible. What was that old saying? No room to swing a cat? And avoiding Sara was going to be next to impossible in such a tight space.

Six or so buckets had been placed strategically on

the scratched lino floor to catch the water dripping down through what was obviously a very leaky tin roof. Up in the exposed rafters, thick filmy cobwebs swayed in the draft from the roaring wind.

"You should have seen it two hours ago," Sara said in a wry voice, indicating a broom and a damp mop resting beside the stove. "The place was filthy."

"I believe you." The strong smell of bleach attacked his nostrils. Darim scratched his chin and turning found a wooden peg to hang his wet clothes on. "No electricity?"

She shook her head. "I'm not sure if that's because the power has been disconnected or because of the storm."

"I'd say it's been a long time before this place had any electricity. Like you said, could be the connection to the grid has been severed. Probably needs rewiring, too. What about running water? A bathroom?"

She marched over to the cupboard where a two-burner gas camper stove had been placed on top. A single gas bottle sat nearby. No doubt she had also brought along the stove. A kettle sat on one of the rings, a thin stream of steam rose into the air.

"No water. There is a water tank out the back but no pump that I could see." Sara waved a hand to the plastic-wrapped carton of 2 litre water bottles sitting on the floor next to the gas bottle. "I brought water with me and just as well. When I turned the tap, nothing but a couple of rusty looking drops emerged. If you go through that rear door, there's a small room tacked onto the back veranda. I think it's meant to be a bathroom but there's only a toilet and a tiny sink."

She shuddered and sent him a loaded glance as she rolled her eyes. "I can't begin to describe what the toilet looked like when I arrived. If it ever worked in the first place, I don't think it had been flushed for at least a century."

He laughed. "I can imagine. I guess we'll have to make do with a porta-potty. I've got one in my four-wheel-drive along with a few other camping items which will be useful. You've been magnificent. I'm sorry I was unable to give you a hand."

"Don't worry, I have a feeling that come tomorrow we are going to find a lot more problems that will need to be addressed sooner rather than later." Sighing, she lifted the singing kettle off the gas hob and onto a stool. "I can make you a cup of tea or coffee? There's nothing else I'm afraid until I can source a fridge and get to the shops."

For a second there, Darim could have sworn her lips trembled. A chink in the stoicism she wore like armour? He didn't blame her as he also felt a tad daunted. It was obvious there would be lot of work ahead of them just to make the shack livable, and she was no doubt tired after ridding the place of dirt and possibly animal droppings. "We."

In the act of crouching down to retrieve a mug from the cupboard, she shot him a narrow glance.

He lifted his eyebrows in a silent challenge. The use

20

of the pronoun '*I*' hadn't escaped him. "*We* will look for a fridge. This is a joint effort, remember?"

"Of course. I hadn't forgotten. Let's discuss the situation tomorrow. I haven't had a chance to digest all the nuts and bolts of this arrangement yet." Straightening, she placed a mug onto the counter next to the portable stove with exaggerated care, filled it with hot water and popped in a tea bag. "First however, we'll need to sort out the sleeping arrangements. Obviously, you will have to bunk down somewhere else."

Darim leaned against the wall. Timber creaked. Wincing, he hoped that the ancient frame would bear his weight, and drawled, "There's plenty of space in the middle of the room for my swag." There wasn't really. She'd have to step over him every time she got out of bed but he couldn't resist teasing her.

Her cheeks pinkened and she pinched her lips together as if annoyed by the betrayal.

His gaze dropped to her mouth and lingered. Was that her natural colour or had she applied lipstick before he'd arrived? And if she had – now *that* was an interesting thought.

"Out of the question. There's hardly room in here for one person to live, certainly not two." Her ink-dark eyes sparked with … outrage? Or could he delude himself and think it was something else?

Awareness of *her* ratcheted up another notch and a heady thrum pulsed through him. This wasn't good. Focus! He wiped his hands down his jeans, trying to rid himself of how good – how right - she'd felt in his arms.

Better remember they were business partners. Anything else and their situation could get messy. And after his divorce, he didn't do messy. Or complicated. Or anything really. Staying single from now on, was the way to go for him.

"One of the rules states we both have to live in the house. I'm sure we can work something out that will suit both of us."

"Your tea." Her dark eyes snapping, she snatched up the mug and held it out. Water slopped over the side onto her hand, and she inhaled sharply.

"I'm a coffee man, myself. But thanks, anyway." Straightening, he crossed over and took the mug. After placing it on the counter, he picked up her hand before she could move away and inspected the red welt where a large blister was beginning to form.

"I don't need your help." She attempted to wriggle out of his grasp.

His grip tightened. "Trust me, blood poisoning is not something you want to experience. Do you have a first-aid kit? I've got one but it's in the car."

"In my bag."

Enclosing his hand around a wrist that felt too thin, too vulnerable, he towed her over to the camp bed. Although she rolled her eyes, she fished out a small canvas bag with a zipper. Taking it from her he quickly located antiseptic cream, gauze and adhesive tape. She stood completely still and silent as he administered aid to the angry-looking burn. So still that it made him wonder what had happened to make her so wary. As he soothed the adhesive strip over the back of her hand, he marvelled over how her skin felt butter soft beneath his touch.

Irritated with the direction of his thoughts, he released his hold rather abruptly and packed away the few items he had used back inside the kit. "There you go. Mind you keep it clean for the next few days. Maybe wear gloves."

For a few seconds neither moved as his gaze meshed with hers. An odd sensation grew. It was if he was being drawn closer. With an almost physical effort, he stepped away, his hands bunched into fists at his sides. He moved to the door, relieved to put some distance between them. Because for a moment there, he had had an insane urge to trace the contours of her face with his fingertips.

Yeah. He definitely was in trouble.

He had to get out of there.

Now.

Darim snatched his coat and hat from the hook before opening the door. A flurry of rain drops smacked him in his face. Rubbing a hand over his eyes, he paused to say, "I'll place the porta-pottie in the bathroom, then get some rack time. See you in the morning, Sara."

Once he had shrugged his wet-weather gear on, he stepped out into the storm and raced to his car. Ignoring the water seeping behind the collar of his coat and trickling down his back, he dealt with the porta-pottie then proceeded to erect his tent. As the wind lashed the canvas, he drove the pegs into the soggy ground all the time reminding himself of what was at stake.

Shared custody of his only child.

Somehow, he'd find a way around this nonsense of joint ownership and turn a broken-down shack into a home.

All he had to do was find a way to get rid of Sara – get her out of the house and out of his life.

CHAPTER 3

The storm crashed and growled like a hungry beast sounding as if it was directly above the leaking roof of Sara's new home. Perched on the edge of her camp bed, she polished off the last mouthful of her three-minute noodles. Wanting to preserve her meagre supply of oil, she'd turned the lantern down as low as possible causing the shadows inside the building to deepen.

She huddled into her only jacket, a second-hand, fleecy-lined parka that she'd purchased at the end of last winter in a jumble sale run by the ladies of Bindarra Creek's Country Women's Association. Her gaze darted about the gloomy room, her ears straining for the slightest indication she had company. She wished she'd thought to bring mice traps with her and decided to add that to her list of 'to-do's' for tomorrow.

As soon as the sun rose, she would read through the paperwork thrust upon her by Ty Devereaux. She'd make notes on what required further clarification and phone the solicitor as soon as she'd finished. Mainly she was keen to discover how she could wiggle out of the joint ownership deal. And then, a trip to the bank which should tell her how much money she could borrow to pay her new partner off. Surely now that she had this property behind her as collateral they would look favourably on an application.

She tossed the empty carton into a spare bucket doing double duty as a rubbish bin then crossed to the sink where she rinsed her spoon using water from the kettle. Another boom of thunder sounded, making the small house shake while rain continued to lash the window. She checked the time; almost eleven. Flexing shoulders stiff from hauling buckets and scrubbing walls and floors, she grabbed the lantern. She moved to the back door then hurried into the tiny bathroom tacked onto the narrow rear veranda. The porta-pottie was a godsend and a wave of gratitude towards her house partner, Darim, flooded over her. After brushing her teeth using some of the bottle of water she'd stashed in there earlier, she went back inside. Circum-navigating the buckets she'd placed on the floor to capture the rain dribbling down from the holes in the roof, she hung her damp parka on a coat hook nailed to the wall. About to turn in for the night, she hesitated.

The storm showed no sign of easing any time soon.

Instead, it seemed to have intensified with a howling wind that rattled the windowpane and the loose fitting timber doors. Anyone outside would not be having a picnic.

Sudden guilt clawed at her heart. She'd insisted there was no room for Darim inside the one-roomed house. He'd made no demur and hadn't argued. Simply, headed out into the wind and rain. What could it hurt for him to sleep on the floor?

She pulled a woolly throw blanket over her shoulders, yanked open the door and held the lantern high.

Wavering yellow light spilled out over deep puddles to reveal Darim sitting on a camp chair under the front flap of a small tent. His head was tucked down low on his chest. He looked so cold, so alone.

So wet.

A bit like a drowned rat. Had he had anything to eat?

I'm so selfish. Before she could change her mind, she stuck two fingers in her mouth and let loose a piercing whistle.

When he looked up squinting a little as the light hit his eyes, she beckoned him forward and shouted, "Sleep inside! It's too wet out here!"

His slow grin was like a heat ray sizzling through her, and her tummy quivered. Already regretting her invitation, she stepped inside, placing the lantern beside the stove. It wasn't long before Darim entered, shaking water in all directions like a wet dog. He had a duffle bag over one shoulder and held something bundled up under his coat which was soon revealed to be his swag.

"Thanks." He placed his coat and hat on the hooks then turned around. "Okay if I bunk down near the wall? That will leave a bit of walk space to the kitchen."

"No worries." Clutching the edges of the blanket together, she hurried over to her camp bed. With his presence the room seemed to shrink, and her thoughts spun to earlier that day when she'd fallen on top of him. She didn't know what was worse: him thinking she was a delicate flower who had hysterics at the sight of a mouse – or the unwanted heat that had simmered through her body at his touch.

Or yet again, the burgeoning need that still lurked deep inside every time her gaze strayed in his direction.

It was loneliness.

Nothing more.

She rubbed at her waist where it was if she could still feel his firm hands – steadying her, reassuring her, protecting her – all those emotions she wanted no part of and was certainly not worthy of receiving. She couldn't tear her eyes from him as he toed off his muddy boots near the door before positioning his swag on the floor.

He was tall but then so were most people given that she was only two inches over five feet. Not bulging with muscles like a gym-junkie, he nevertheless obviously kept himself fit as revealed when he pulled off his sweater. His black tee-shirt moulded to a taut abdomen and firm upper arm muscles. Not strictly handsome and certainly nowhere near a 'pretty-boy', his well-cut features coupled with a square chin radiated a strength of character that was more appealing. At least to her.

Awareness rippled, her skin prickled, and a very unwelcome ache bloomed in places she had locked away years ago. Or was it a need? How long had it been since she'd enjoyed warmth and companionship? How long since she'd experienced ... love?

Drawing a slow breath, she attempted to ease the sudden racing of her pulse as she scooted across the bed, putting as much distance as she could between them. Her back pressed to the wall, she picked up the folder in hands that felt like they'd turned into jelly and forced herself to read the first page.

"Anything we should know about?" His smoothly modulated voice broke into her jumbled thoughts, and she jumped a little.

When she glanced up, she caught his considering gaze. He was sitting cross-legged on his swag and rubbing his damp hair with a towel. Those mocha dark eyes of his had not missed her startled reaction. Now she was well and truly cemented in his mind as nervy, maybe even someone who would need looking after twenty-four-seven. And that was not her.

Her former life as an inner-city cop meant she'd not only experienced but handled plenty of hairy situations. Then, of course, had come the exposure of her terrible mistake to her friends and parents. And her fellow officers. She'd diminished herself in their eyes and fully deserved the punishment that had been dealt. Another brutal lesson that had toughened her outer shell so much that sometimes in the early hours of the morning, she wondered if the person she had once been was dead and buried for all time.

"Not as yet." She could hardly fess up that not even one word had sunk into her brain.

"Mmm. My suggestion is that we seek alternate legal advice."

"Bit late now. We both signed that document," she couldn't refrain from pointing out.

Her snarky tone earned a hard stare from his end. "True. However, I hardly believe that you're keen to live hand-to-jowl with a strange man for the next twelve months. I want to check exactly how water-tight those conditions actually are in case there's room to manoeuvre. No need to put either of us through any undue … inconvenience." For some reason, his smooth voice and reasonable explanation only served to irk.

"Since Ty is the only solicitor in town these days, I suppose you'll be making a trip to a larger town? Like Newcastle? Sydney?" And hopefully that would keep him away for more than forty-eight hours!

Darim folded the damp towel into a perfect rectangle before lying down on his swag and linking his hands behind his head. Merriment oozed from his twinkling eyes and his lips tipped upwards. "Trying to get rid of me? Sorry, honey. That is so not going to work. I need this house."

"Well, so do I!" hissed Sara from between gritted teeth. Drat the man. "And my name is Sara."

"My apologies. Sara."

Uncertain whether she felt annoyed or amused or childish or maybe all three, she clamped her mouth shut.

"Good night," he said quietly.

Without taking another look at him, Sara reached over and extinguished the lantern. Yawning, she curled into the throw rug. She squeezed her eyes shut but no matter how hard she tried, his wicked smile stayed with her as she drifted off. All she could hope for was that he would remain out of her dreams.

TRIUMPH FLOODED through Sara as she was presented with the award for the best hand-woven llama rug of the year; the same one which was displayed in all its rich reds, vibrant yellows and deep azure-blue glory on the wall behind the podium.

Applause vibrated. Paparazzi flashed lights and clicked cameras. Hammering pounded.

Hang on – *hammering*?

Frowning, she attempted to stay immersed in the wonderful sensations of success and achievement. As she wriggled on the narrow camp bed, she began to sink back into her dream.

The sudden piercing screech of a high-pitched power tool sliced into her head. The last remnants of sleep along with all those feel-good emotions scattered in all directions like a flock of startled pigeons.

Opening her eyes, she stared blankly at the shadowy rafters above her head. A flurry of dust drifted down as something grey and furry dashed along a beam then with arms outstretched glided through the air to land on top of the stove. A pair of dark, round glistening eyes looked at her. A possum. Now that she could deal with. But that teeth-rattling noise was quite another thing. She pushed to her feet and the possum leapt to the floor before dashing out of the open door.

The open door.

And she knew exactly who had left it open! Probably hoping that she would scream and panic at the sight of the cute specimen of wildlife that had entered the shack while she'd been sleeping. Wincing, she pushed back a tangle of hair from her face with an impatient hand as the clamour from outside reached new peaks. After one brisk tug at her top, she marched across the small room and onto the rear verandah.

"Sorry. I hope I didn't wake you," called a deep, smooth-as-whipped-molasses voice that was becoming far too familiar to her ears.

Barring her teeth, her gaze fixed on the man welding the power tool. "Of course not. I always like to get an early start to the day."

"Same." He smiled.

She knew a fake smile when she saw one and flashed one of her own.

Their eyes met and clashed as they traded glares.

Gauntlet thrown down.

He gave a brief nod.

And accepted.

It seemed she wasn't the only one with the idea of getting rid of her opponent. She clamped her mouth shut over the frustration she wanted so badly to vent. He couldn't possibly know how much having a place of her own meant; or how this could be her only chance of a fresh start. While, judging by the latest model Land Rover he drove – hell, he could probably buy a house anywhere. He didn't have to have this one.

His narrowed stare finally left her face and travelled south, taking his sweet time to inspect her person. He appeared to linger on her bare feet. "You need to put some boots on. Or at least shoes of some kind. There are a lot of snakes around this time of year."

Her toes curled and something hot and heavy churned in her belly as his hooded gaze wandered back to hers. She should have thrown her parka over the thin tank top and shorts she wore. Or a blanket. Or anything that would cover her exposed skin and obvious reaction to his perusal. She folded her arms in the futile hope she could hide her peaking nipples.

He grinned.

Then winked.

Cheeky sod.

Whirling around, she stormed through the shack. After making use of the bathroom, she dressed into a sky-blue tee-shirt and a pair of sand-coloured cargo pants before tidying the small shack. Longing for her usual caffeine hit, she put water on to boil then found her socks and boots. She debated with herself, then with a shrug made two mugs of black coffee which she carried outside.

Darim hadn't let up making a racket. He didn't stop working when she walked over the patch of weeds, skirting the puddles leftover from the storm.

"Coffee." She held out the mug. "It's black. Sorry, I never thought to ask if you wanted milk. I always have mine without."

He glanced up, turned off the drill before placing it onto the soggy ground. "Thanks." His smile this time held genuine appreciation and she couldn't help the tiny flutter of pleasure it caused.

A little civilized conversation couldn't hurt.

"What are you doing?" She took a sip, almost closing her eyes at the hot, bitter tang.

Darim swallowed a mouthful of his own coffee then gave a satisfied sigh. "Exactly how I like it – seriously, thanks. I didn't make one earlier as I didn't want to disturb you."

She arched a brow and considered him over the rim of her mug. "Really? And what was with the open door and all the noise you've been making? As if that wouldn't disturb me."

He laughed. "Touche. I'm repairing the pump for the water tank. I've already put a call through to the electricity company. Someone should be out here later today to test the power pole connection at the road. If that's okay, then the problem is here at the house. Either way, we'll have to find an electrician." He paused to drink more of his coffee. "The place will need to be re-wired. The fuse box at the very least is a mess."

Sara leaned against the side of his 4WD. "Any idea of the cost?"

Darim shrugged. "None. Making this place habitable won't be cheap."

With her thoughts centered on her all but empty bank account, she didn't respond as she enjoyed the last of her coffee and stared into the distance. Admitting her lack of funds seemed shameful, as if she had failed – yet again. But how to explain? Especially to a near stranger. Her shoulders slumped as the feeling of being totally inadequate weighed her down.

Beside her, Darim drained the last of his coffee and popped the empty mug onto the bonnet of his Land Rover. Reaching through the open passenger window, he retrieved a familiar-looking folder and opened it.

Although it had yet to reach seven o'clock, the early morning sun still packed quite a punch. Heat and soupy humidity pulsed in the still air, enriching the lemony scents of the surrounding bushland. Hard to believe that last night she had been wearing a parka. With the storm blown over, the day promised to be a typical hot summer's day. The list of chores that waited was innumerable – the cost of which she couldn't begin to estimate. A small sigh escaped, and she transferred her gaze to the bottom of her mug.

Empty. Just like her pockets.

Darim rustled paper as if he was trying to gain her attention.

She looked up.

He was staring at her.

Was that concern she read in his velvety brown eyes?

Or pity?

She pushed away from the vehicle. Her spine snapped straight, and she lifted her chin. She didn't need his pity. Or his concern. Or his … anything. She'd do this, find a way to make it work. On her own. Like she always did.

She'd succeed – and with success, she would eradicate her shameful past - forever.

CHAPTER 4

F or a moment there Sara looked…forlorn. Alone. Lost.

Darim's fingers trembled and one of the pages he held fluttered to the ground. Bending, he scooped it up and replaced it inside the folder. He had to keep his mind on the end goal - a house – no, *his* house. A permanent place for him and Skye to put down roots, to call home. Still, he couldn't banish the itch deep inside to wrap his arms around the delicate-looking woman in front of him and offer what comfort he could. Tell her, everything was going to be all right. That he would take care of it. And her.

Damnit.

He didn't need that kind of complication. He didn't want it. Celeste had soured him on relationships – at least in the short term. What was important in his life now, was cementing the bond between him and Skye.

Sara would have to fend for herself.

Besides, that militant gleam that had just appeared in her eyes told him louder than words, she would repulse any move on his part to step past the barriers that lay between them. He inwardly rolled his eyes at the anticipation that sparked and crackled like live electricity. He'd always enjoyed a challenge. Besting Sara, he was beginning to realise would be quite an achievement. And even though he wanted to deny it existed, there was a powerful sexual attraction between them.

He captured her intense gaze, absorbing the thrill that danced and teased along his nerve ends. Hell yeah. What harm could a little flirtation do while he plotted against her? He'd keep it casual. Maybe even a few kisses here and there. With him controlling the pace and being well and truly burned from Celeste, there was no chance his heart would be at risk.

Confidence swelled and he smiled, enjoying the wary expression that flittered across her face. Yep. This was going to be fun. And he couldn't wait to get started.

Thank heavens though, that she had changed out of her far-too-sexy and flimsy sleepwear.

"I read through the information Ty provided." He ran a hand along his raspy jaw, grinning as her gaze tracked his movement and she swallowed. "As you've probably already figured out, we can't extend the living area of the house, or we forfeit our windfall. However, I still think we should take separate legal advice. I intend to scan the document and email it to my solicitor in Sydney. I suggest you do the same."

He paused but Sara didn't respond. It was possible she didn't have the means to fund alternate advice. He made a mental note to ensure that if his legal team found anything helpful he'd pass it on. He wanted her gone but he always played fair. "In the meantime, I reckon there's nothing stopping us putting a caravan on the property and one of us living in that while the other occupies the house. We then share the cooking and bathroom facilities."

As if woken at the word *'cooking'*, his stomach grumbled reminding him he'd missed dinner the night before; and he certainly didn't miss his companion's sidelong glance directed towards his middle.

"I guess that sounds like a good plan." A little frown wrinkled her forehead.

He rushed to reassure. "I'll provide the caravan and will live in it. The only thing is…" Now it was his turn to frown. "Look. I'll be honest here. I need somewhere decent for my daughter to stay. I'm not certain that Celeste – that's my ex – will agree that a caravan will cut it. Unless it's some massive contraption and even then, she may be picky. She's a bit of a snob that way. Wouldn't have a bar on holidaying in caravans when we were together. If she puts her foot down, that means another Christmas I miss out on."

"You could still get a caravan but say your daughter is sleeping inside the house. If we get single bunk beds, that shouldn't take up any more floor space than what my camp bed occupies. Plus, there's the chest of drawers I brought with me. Your daughter could lay a few of her things on the top. A friend of mine, Dodge, may even have some second-hand bunks in his shop." Sara placed her fingertips on his forearm. The brief touch seemed to burn through to his very bone. When she moved away, his skin continued to tingle.

"That could work. I can send the ex a snap of the front of the house plus the bunk beds and I could imply that area is Skye's bedroom. No way will she have any idea of the actual size of the place. Unless she bothers to check it out herself, she won't be none the wiser. I can't see her leaving her city life for a jaunt in the country, no matter how short." Even he could hear the relief – and hope - in his voice.

He shot Sara an uncertain glance. Hell, had he just given her ammunition to shoot him down? One whisper from her to Celeste and all his dreams would go up in flames.

But Sara gave no indication she had any such thoughts. Rather, her face had brightened and there was no trace of the worried frown she'd displayed a few moments ago. Maybe she liked the idea of a pre-teen running around. He pretended to flick over a few pages while his mind raced. Unless his memory was faulty – and that hardly ever happened – she had mentioned yesterday that she had no living relatives. How sad and lonely that must be, to know there was no one of your own blood in the world.

As if she'd read his thoughts, she asked, "How old is

your daughter?"

"Skye turned twelve a couple of weeks ago. Her mother took her out to dinner at some fancy restaurant to celebrate." He had to force himself not to roll his eyes. If he'd had his way, his daughter would have gone to the zoo with her friends, or something similar. Something fun. But no, the choice would have been Celeste's idea of 'fun'. "I wasn't able to get leave to see her."

At her questioning glance, he added, "I'm a Major, currently attached to the new Army Training Facility down the road."

"Is it a permanent posting?"

For a second he squinted at the sun glowing gold and bright through the trees blanketing the horizon as his mind churned over the million-dollar question that had nagged him these past months. "That's my intention although I've been tossing up the idea of retiring from the military. But after twenty-five years of service, it's all I know. What the devil would I do with myself?" He shrugged.

"It's never too late to start again." Her voice was low but firm.

"You really think so?" He turned and examined her expression, but although her eyelashes flickered at his scrutiny, not a nuance crossed her face.

"I know so." She raised her head and met his gaze full-on.

"Okaaay," he drew the single word out.

An odd connection pulsed to life between them; it was as if his soul recognised her.

Shifting the folder to one hand, Darim reached out and traced a gentle finger along the curve of her jaw. She didn't move away; maybe she was as entranced in the moment as much as he was. The thought was downright disturbing. Even more so, was his realisation that he didn't care.

A mobile blared to life, and the link severed.

"Yours I believe." Sara pushed off from the Land Rover and, retrieving both mugs, walked back to the shack.

With his eyes fixed on her retreating figure, Darim pulled out his phone.

"Darim? It's me. Celeste."

"No sweat."

"You are such a dick," she snapped nastily. "I need to make plans for the holidays." She gave a little giggle and her voice turned smug. "Antoine has suggested we spend Christmas in Paris. If you haven't gotten a house organised, then I'm sending Skye to my stay with my brother in Melbourne."

He scowled. Celeste's brother was unmarried and led quite a flamboyant lifestyle. No way was his daughter going anywhere near that partying yobo. Still, he couldn't stop the jib bursting from his mouth. "Somehow I'm not surprised that you don't want your daughter cramping your style."

"She's your daughter too. I thought you wanted to spend more time with her?" Her pitch rose.

"I do. And I've been working on it. Actually, I'm glad you called." He paused and scrutinised the old house. Yep. One wall had quite a lean to it. And was that another mouse running along the broken floor-boards of the verandah? Bulldozing the decrepit building to the ground would be a relief. But those blasted stipulations. He – and Sara – would just have to work with what they had. Which meant a rosy and very blurry picture would have to be painted for his ex.

"I've got a house. Give me a couple of days, and I'll have everything ready for Skye. Her own sleeping quarters even." Well, that part was true – in a way if you weren't too picky.

The word quarters could mean anything so he wasn't really lying.

"A house? What? Where? Last time I heard, you were moaning how there were no …"

Pretending he hadn't heard her stuttering, he cut in. "Bunk beds, a cupboard for her clothes. Plenty of room for her to play and for her cousins to visit."

"Huh. Fatima!"

"Yes. She *is* my sister," he gritted out.

"Your half-sister."

"Bloody hell, Celeste. Get over it. Now that I've delivered, it's your turn. What day will Skye be arriv-ing? Or do you want me to drive down and pick her up?"

"I need to make sure this house of yours is suitable."

He all but ground his teeth. "I'll send photos when I

43

have a spare minute. I have a house and you therefore have no grounds to deny me access. Well?"

Her sigh came down the line, long and heavy as if the one simple thing of sending their daughter some-where would be a Herculean feat for her. "I prefer you stay completely away from my new life. That was the agreement, remember? She can be in Armidale on the 5th, at six o'clock in the afternoon. You can pick her up from the train station."

"Sounds like you already had it arranged."

"Do you want her there, or not?"

"I'll be there." His voice warmed. "Tell Skye, I'm looking forward to seeing her."

"Tell her yourself." She hung up.

Darim glared at the phone, then with a sigh, put the damn thing back in his pocket. No use losing his cool, nothing would ever change Celeste. Picking up the drill, he went back to work. In less than half an hour, he had the hole in the side of the water tank patched and had fixed the pump. At least, he hoped he had but until the electricity was back on, he had no way of knowing for sure. He packed his tools in the back of his 4WD and headed to the house. While he had been working, he had been aware of Sara coming back and forth. First, emptying buckets, and then bringing out a mop to dry, then draping towels and a few washcloths over the veranda railing.

As he passed through the open door, she looked over her shoulder from where she was scrubbing a peculiar-looking stain on the floor.

"What's up? Would you like another coffee?"

"No, thanks."

She straightened. "I have muesli and long-life milk, although only almond, if you'd like something to eat."

"Hell yeah. That would be fantastic." He smiled as he popped his slouch hat onto the hook and wiped sweat from his forehead with the back of his hand. Only nine o'clock and already the interior of the shack was like an oven. "I thought we could head into town shortly. See if we can buy that furniture you mentioned. And we need a fridge before we head to the supermarket. I'll pay and keep a tab. We can talk about how we'll deal with the money side of things later."

After a long considering moment, she said, "Alright. I'm all for making this place more habitable as soon as possible." Sara poured the cereal into a plastic bowl and added a liberal splash of milk, before replacing the items in the cupboard. She handed him the bowl and a spoon.

"Thanks." He dived right into his breakfast, while Sara put her gloves back on.

"Did you know there was a possum in here this morning?"

"Yeah, I saw the little fella hanging about. I admit, I was surprised not to hear a scream." Chuckling, he crossed over and rinsed his now empty bowl with the remainder of the water in the kettle. He picked up a bottle of water. He held it up and when she nodded, he broke the cap and drank.

"Anything but mice I'm fine with." She returned to her scrubbing.

He set down the empty bottle. "Good to know. I'll remember that."

"We need an electrician," she reminded him.

"I hadn't forgotten. My sister may know of someone. She's been living here for a few years now."

"Probably lucky if we get someone here by Christmas." Sara snorted as she tossed the scourer into a bucket of soapy water and ripped off the rubber gloves she was wearing. Moisture gleamed on her skin giving her face a youthful dewiness he found quite disarming.

Dewiness! What the devil was happening to him?

"I agree, which means we'll have to make ourselves self-sufficient."

Leaning against the cupboard, she folded her arms and arched one thin dark brow. "What do you suggest?" Her smile was a trifle crooked, and he wanted to trace the outline of her lips with his fingers.

He stuffed his hands into his pants pockets where they could be trusted. "My daughter will be here on the 5th," he said abruptly.

"We'll have to move fast then. Let's make a list." She walked to where her duffle bag was placed at the end of the camp bed and pulled out a small notebook and pen. When she sat down on the bed, he joined her, careful to keep the full length between them. "Right. Beds, table, chairs, food and more drinking water of course, and we need a fridge. But that can probably wait until we have the power on." She scribbled on the pad.

"Agree. I can knock up a timber cubicle for an outdoor shower. So put that down. Is there a hardware store in town?"

"Yes. The Handy Hammer. It's quite a big store nowadays since the owners moved premises. They've got a decent building section."

"That's great. Let's see ... I've got folding solar panels for limited power plus a bush shower bag we can use. I'd like to drop in at the caravan park and see if there is a van I can hire."

"Doubtful. The town is chock full of tourists and your army mates' relatives for Christmas. You may have to go to Armidale or Tamworth for that one." She shot him a grin full of mischief. "You'll need a Christmas tree for your daughter if you want to make this visit special."

He rubbed his hands together. "Add that to the list and include Christmas lights and decorations. I thought an outdoor dining setting would be best. What with it being summer, plus the lack of space. And a couch and a telly would be good."

That surprised a laugh from her. "Where do you think we can fit a couch? This place is so small."

"It can go against the side wall when my swag is out of the way."

She made a note in the book. "We can check the second-hand furniture section in the local gazette if Dodge doesn't have anything in stock. Could pick up some bargains."

Her suggestion merely cemented his certainty that

her bank balance was low – if she had anything at all. If he dared mention such a thing however, she would probably bite his head off. He was enjoying their easy conversation too much to want to tarnish their surprising rapport. "Agreed."

She nibbled the end of the pen and he had to push aside thoughts of her nibbling something else entirely. "If we can't source a couch in the short term, what about some hammocks? There's plenty of trees we can hang them from. If this heat continues, sleeping outside may be our only option unless we want to roast ourselves like a Sunday dinner."

Grinning, he clapped a hand to her shoulder. "Now, we're talking. Nothing like teamwork for getting a job done in record time."

Her shuttered eyes met his. "I'm not on your team." She surged to her feet, neatly tucking the notebook into a pocket on her cargo pants. "Let's move. I suggest we go in separate cars. We'll accomplish more that way. Plus, I have a couple of personal errands to run. I'll check out Dodge's shop, while you deal with the hardware side of things."

"It's not a race," he said mildly.

"No. But I happen to have better things to do with my time, than spend them fooling about with you."

"Ouch. That hurt."

"It was meant to." Her voice was sharp but the glance she sent over her shoulder as she picked up a fabric handbag with long handles, glimmered with laughter. She marched out the door like she was on a mission.

He ambled after her, snatching up his hat as he passed. Palming his hips, he waited in the yard as she climbed into her car, an old Holden ute that seemed to be covered with more rust than paintwork. A few seconds later, no engine roared to life. Rather came the grinding groan of a flat battery.

He had to smile as he saw her lay her head on the steering wheel for a moment.

Not his doing. But still – yesterday he would have done it for sure if he had thought of it. Today? Today - everything felt different.

With uneasiness stabbing at his nerve ends as if he was embarking on a military campaign, he moved to her car and opened the passenger door. Leaning down, he said, "I could give you a jump start but I don't have any jump leads. Come on. We'll take the Land Rover, but first let's check what size battery you need, and we can get one when we're in town." He didn't miss the grimace that crossed her face and he had to bite back the offer to pay for it. Somehow, he just knew she wouldn't accept what she would see as charity – certainly not from him. She popped the hood, and he noted the details of the battery. Then went to his own vehicle and waited until she clambered in the other side. "Ready?"

Wordless, she nodded, face set and turned resolutely away from him. She snapped on her seatbelt.

Anger rose. Did she think he was responsible? Or

was she one of those sulky types, like his ex, who had a tantrum when life didn't work their way?

No sooner had those thoughts entered his head, then they disappeared along with his brief flare of annoyance. She was worried. Possibly embarrassed. He knew with a deep certainty that it was because she wasn't flush with money.

That meant if her finances were so limited, he'd be the one forking out the dough so they could both have a modicum of comfort this Christmas. He put the Land Rover into gear and drove down the rutted track.

She'd owe him.

She'd be in his debt.

Maybe he could utilise that to his advantage. He tapped his forefinger on the wheel and frowned. Somehow his plan to oust her from his life and their shared inheritance had lost its appeal. For the first time, he wondered why she wanted – no needed – the house so … so desperately. He had opened up about his daughter, but Sara had remained close-lipped.

Change of plans.

Discover Sara's reasons. And just maybe there would be a way he could use it to his advantage.

CHAPTER 5

The drive into town wasn't far, but it was long enough for that prickly tension to grow and grow so much that Sara was about to jump from the car when they finally passed the old brewery. Ahead and on the left was the SES building, then the vicarage where, in the front yard, a plastic green tree had been liberally adorned with Christmas decorations. Streams of toilet paper dangled from the branches and hung limp under the hot summer sun. A small lean-to that looked as if the slightest breeze would blow it over had been positioned next to the tree. She could just make out a couple of stone statues bookending a real baby's crib where wisps of straw protruded. A lone discarded bedroom slipper lay discarded and forgotten half-way down the driveway.

"He's been diagnosed with dementia, you know," she said.

"Who? That's tough for him and his family."

"Mr. Miller. Actually, I'm not sure what to call him these days. He used to be the vicar in Bindarra Creek until he became too unwell to continue. Now his wife wears the clerical collar, and he assists her during services." She blew out a shaky breath. Dementia was far to close to home. Her own parents had suffered from Parkinson's disease dementia. Her cheeks heated as she sensed the glance Darim threw her way. Nodding towards the display, she said, "Everyone is really getting into the Christmas spirit this year. Did you hear that there is a competition running for the best decorated house?"

"Maybe we should enter."

She looked over at him and caught his cheeky grin. That intriguing dimple peeped beside his mouth. "Now that would be a challenge."

He laughed.

Suddenly the stress over her lack of finances ebbed away and the day seemed brighter. Who would have thought his company would be so enjoyable? Or how appealing she found his quiet air of assurance? He didn't appear to be one for idle chitchat – rather he spoke only when he had something significant to say. He seemed to be a man secure in his own skin. And then there was his relaxed and yet alert attitude. She didn't know what to make of how comfortable she felt in his presence. It took quite an effort for her to remind herself that, in a way, he was her enemy. The one standing between her and a future of financial success.

But maybe having him around wouldn't be the problem she had first thought.

Maybe joint ownership was something she could work with.

"Where to first?" Darim slowed the car.

"The hardware shop – in case they need to order in the timber you need. Then I thought we could park in the Riverside Pub's parking lot and head to Dodge's shop."

"Excellent strategy."

Her heart fluttered at the sidelong smile he sent her way. She remained in the car while he dealt with the timber and whatever else he needed. Half an hour later he was back and they continued their cruise through the bustling streets. Despite the increasing heat, the footpaths were packed with people. The shop fronts as they passed, glowed and glittered with festive decorations. A massive pine tree near the Main Street side of Lette Park was in the process of being decorated, with men manning ladders and others passing up long *'ropes'* of Christmas fairy lights.

"I've told you why securing a house is so important to me. How about you? Why were you so … keen to sign on the dotted line and put up with these kooky conditions?"

Her heart stuttered. How much to reveal? Not even Dodge, who she considered to be her closest friend in Bindarra Creek, knew the full extent of her dreams or her determination. But then she had never been one who was fully comfortable about sharing her innermost thoughts with others. She ran her tongue over her dry lower lip. "I want to set up a home business selling hand-woven llama rugs, pillows and wall-hangings. Which means I need a place with some land." No need to admit the humiliation of how the bank had turned her down too many times to count. And certainly, no need to reveal how much this fresh start meant to her.

"Wow. That sounds fascinating. Will you need your own animals?"

"Already got that sorted. Well, a start anyway." Excitement enthused warmth into her voice. Forgetting for a moment that he was her opponent, she turned to him. "I've been working towards this idea for the past couple of years. I've got two young female crias and a male cria that are agisted on Grady Ferguson's land. He's got a farm a few k's out of town."

His approving smile caused her heart to swell. "What a great idea. You'll be your own boss. I'm sure you'll make a success of it. I bet you'll want to get your animals moved home as soon as possible."

Home.

It had been a long, long time since Sara had had a real home. Her eyes stung. She widened them so no betraying tears would fall. Unable to speak for a second she simply nodded.

Darim switched his attention back to his driving. "Let's make that a priority. I've already put an order in for fencing wire and posts which will be delivered tomorrow. I reckon if we work together, we'll have one paddock even if it's a small one ready in a couple of days' time. I'll ring through another order later today for more timber and we'll erect a lean-to for them as well." He spoke in a casual fashion, and she knew he'd spotted her momentary display of weakness.

He was kind.

A trait Sara didn't often come across.

When he pulled up outside *'Phoenix Restorations and Antiques',* she all but launched herself out of his vehicle.

The interior of the shop was blessedly cool after the heat from the blazing sun outside. Sara's spirits lifted as she spotted Tessa wrapping a mosaic lamp in Christmas paper, while her grandmother-in-law sat on a stool hunched over something on the reception counter. Both looked up as Sara wound her way through the jumble of furniture and ornaments crowding the store.

"Sara. Would you like some iced tea?" Smiling, Tessa set aside the lamp and reached for a tall jug reposing on a bamboo serving platter. Without waiting for a response, she poured out two glasses. "And one for your … friend." Her eyes sparkled with a mixture of feminine interest and curiosity as she pushed the glasses in their direction.

Cheeks hot, Sara mumbled. "This is Darim Cooper. Darim, meet Tessa Myers and Ms. Lette. My mate Dodge's wife and his grandmother. They also own and run a bed and breakfast called Fig Tree Lodge which is one of the town's most historical buildings."

Ms. Lette said, "Don't forget Matilda."

Sara whispered, "It's supposed to be haunted by Ms. Lette's great aunt."

"No suppose about it. It's a fact." Edwina Lette took a noisy slurp of her own iced tea and sent Darim an inquisitive stare. She took her time looking him over. "I knew it."

From experience, Sara clamped her mouth tight not wanting to open that particular can of worms.

However, Darim stepped right into the trap. "Knew what, ma'am?"

"What a peach. I always admire a man who's respectful," purred Ms. Lette. She set her glass down and turned over another tarot card.

Sara couldn't stop her gaze from landing on the card – *the lovers*.

"Ah hah! I've been expecting you, Darim." Edwina Lette tapped the card, while Sara wished for a Tardis to whisk her to another planet.

Darim cleared his throat.

When Sara snuck a peek at him, amusement flared. Even though he had olive skin, there was no mistaking his flushed face. Good to know she wasn't the only one embarrassed.

"What have you been up to, Sara?" Eyes as bright and sharp as the sun, Edwina stared at them both. "I hear you visited the solicitor's office yesterday."

There was no escaping the Bindarra Creek telegraph. Just about everyone in town probably knew about the bequest by now, and heaven only knew how wild the speculations were and how much the entire affair had been blown out of proportion. She gave a quick abbreviated re-cap of the bequest, waited a few beats until the gasps and well-wishing had died down then said, "We need a few pieces of furniture." Then a thought struck her, and she added ever faster, "Nothing fancy."

Tessa nodded and said smoothly, "You're both in luck, we've got a sale on this week. Dodge went to Tamworth recently and came back with so many items that we can't fit them in the shop."

"Bunk beds?" Sara asked. "Maybe a couch. A dining table and a few chairs?"

"I'm sure we can fill any order at the moment." Smiling, Tessa spread her hands wide to encompass the packed shop. "By the way, are you still okay to pick up that package for me next week?"

"I haven't forgotten. As soon as my shift at the hospital finishes, I'll be all over it."

"Thanks, Sara."

"What's this all about?" Ms. Lette pinned her piercing stare on her granddaughter-in-law.

"Nothing important, Gran. What with pre-school closing early for the holidays, I'll have Tilly under my feet while I'm minding the shop, so I asked Sara to help out. Now about that furniture."

Darim spoke up. "An outdoor setting would be preferable rather than a formal dining table. Any chance of a TV? I know that's going to be the second thing my daughter will ask about – first will be internet connection."

"She sounds exactly like my eldest! Walk this way." Tessa grinned and began to head to the back of the store.

"Don't forget our bike ride on Tuesday, Sara. And bring your eye-candy with you. We could do with another hottie in our riding group," Ms. Lette called.

Sara gave the elderly lady a brief smile, and aware of Ms. Lette's glittering eagle eyes on her back, did her best not to glance in Darim's direction. But there was no mistaking his amused chuckle or the quiet resonance of his voice as he confirmed details of the bike ride with that wicked old lady. She'd been looking forward to the ride and swim at a local waterhole. Now it appeared she'd be spending more time with him. So much for keeping a low profile.

She caught up with Tessa who was waiting at the rear of the building. Through the open door she could see the glint of the Akuna River between the swaying branches of a willow tree. Above the doorway a bunch of green and white mistletoe bound by a ruby-red ribbon dangled and gently rocked side to side in the slight breeze.

"If you have no one to kiss, then make a wish." Tessa grinned as she waved a hand towards the decoration. "It's a Christmas tradition."

Sara frowned a little. "Really? I've never heard of it."

"It's true, according to Scarlett Stark. She's a midwife at the hospital and really into Christmas. Either way, a Christmas wish never goes astray. But apparently, you're only allowed one each year."

Tessa disappeared into another room off to the left.

About to follow, Sara hesitated as she considered the mistletoe. She'd always felt Christmas to be a magical time of year. A time when anything could happen. One of her first memories was of a Christmas Day and her parents leading her into their tiny living room. They had urged her to close her eyes and not open them until they told her to. When they'd cried out, *'Open!'*, she'd squealed with delight at the colourfully wrapped presents under the small tree. Her mother had said how hard they had worked to emigrate to this country they now called their new home. She'd said how life was like Christmas; if you worked hard enough, wished hard enough, then anything could come true.

Tears burned behind her eyes and Sara swallowed over the lump clogging her throat. How she missed her parents. How she wished she had spent more time with them before it was too late.

How she wished she'd never brought shame on them.

If she became successful in her business then maybe, somehow, that could expunge her mistake and even though they were gone, she could still make them proud. Afterall, their sole dream was for their only child to achieve prestige and respect.

The hot breeze pushed against Sara's face, whipping her hair in her eyes and sending the mistletoe jumping like a puppet on strings.

And Sara made her wish.

CHAPTER 6

Mending the fences over the next few days, proved more difficult than either Sara or Darim had imagined. First, there had been a delay with the delivery. Then their order was mixed up with someone else's. Then when it finally arrived, doing the actual work itself had been a bit of an eye-opener as neither had any experience with working on a property. The first week of summer's intense heat, hadn't helped coupled with the fact that locating a second-hand fridge in good working order had been next to impossible – so far. The only bright note had been when an electrician had turned up on Sunday afternoon and re-wired the small house.

At least they now had lights, running water and a flushing toilet, although they were still using the bush shower Darim had set up – not that Sara complained. Any shower, even if it was tepid water was a blessing after long days patching holes in the tin roof and old timber walls, re-wiring fences and building a lean-to in the closest paddock.

She couldn't fault her new housemate.

Darim worked hard. Never whinged and always seemed to be cheerful no matter how hot the day. He never showed any frustration or anger when a new problem presented itself. Simply, talked it over with Sara in a calm voice and together they found a solution.

They had set up a pair of bunk beds in the corner where Sara had previously situated her camp bed and which she had given to Darim for use in his tent. With new cotton sheets, orange butterfly covered doonas, and a couple of yellow and white throw cushions, the beds looked welcoming and exactly what a young girl would love. A three-seater couch with squishy cushions and made from ice grey fabric had been squeezed against one wall. A boxy television set sat on an upturned milk crate. Reception out there was spotty to say the least but hopefully Darim's daughter would be too busy outside to want to watch TV.

Tessa had thrown in a rug for the floor and with an outdoor wooden table and bench seats to eat on, the place had begun to feel more homely. Although she suspected Tessa had lowered her prices for Sara's benefit, she had decided not to argue and accept in the spirit of friendship.

They had split the costs down the middle with Darim keeping track of their expenses and giving Sara unlimited time to pay her share. After another disappointing appointment with the bank's loan officer, she had admitted that she would have to reimburse him each week when she was paid for her work at the hospital. He didn't quibble. Not once did he propose they buy brand new either. Sara had eagerly accepted some of Vince Stark's shifts at the hospital since he was on stress leave. This had helped restore her cash flow a tad but left her feeling exhausted after such long days on her feet. One blessing was that after the past couple of years of regularly rainfall, the paddocks were chock a block full of good feed for her llamas.

As the days passed, they settled into an easy, if some-what guarded, working pattern; both determined to have as much established as possible in the quickest time frame.

Of course, Darim's motivation was the imminent arrival of his daughter. For Sara, she wanted her llamas where she could see them. Having them close by, somehow made her goal of a successful business more of a reality than a pipe dream.

On Monday morning, she woke to the tantalising scent of hot coffee and frying bacon. She scrambled to her feet, rubbing her eyes for a moment before pulling back the Japanese paper screen dividing the small sleeping area from the rest of the room.

With his back still to her, Darim stood beside the camp stove. "Morning, Sara. I've got good news. My sister, Fatima, has a fridge for us. I've also located a caravan. Bad news, the caravan is in Armidale." He shot a quick smile over his shoulder. "I'll pick the van up when I go to get Skye this afternoon. Thought I'd leave a bit early, say tennish to give myself time to make sure I'm happy with its condition. Sorry. I know you wanted to get your llamas here today."

"It's okay. Another day won't matter. Although, I could walk them here myself." She swallowed a yawn and fiddled with the edge of a ragged band aid that covered yet another scratch from the wire fence.

Setting the pan down, he turned around and pointed the spatula at her. "I just had a thought. Why not wait until tomorrow? Skye would love to help out."

Sara smiled. "That's a great idea however tomorrow isn't good for me. I'm committed to a bike ride to the rock pool at Ward's Gully."

His eyebrows rose and a wide grin spread over his face. "I remember. That nice old lady invited me, too."

Damn. She'd hoped he'd forgotten all about it. Sara ducked her head as she recalled that blasted tarot card Edwina Lette had laid out on the reception counter in Dodge's store. *The lovers. No. Way. Ever.* "Your daughter will be here. Besides, won't you need a bike? Or rather two bikes?" She tossed off as many objections as she could think of.

"Now. Now. Someone needs her coffee. Come on over, I've got your mug ready and waiting." He turned back to the stove and began to pile a couple of plates with bacon and fried eggs. "You won't be so grouchy once you have food in your stomach." Picking up the plates, he walked out the door.

Sara made quick use of the bathroom, gave herself a

liberal spray of deodorant and donned a pair of cotton shorts and a tee. About to leave the house, her gaze fell on the folder from the solicitor. What if she could trick Darim into staying away from the house? What was that clause again? Something about forfeiting their claim if they were away from the property? She snatched up the folder and almost ripped the pages apart as she riffled through them until she found what she was looking for. There. Twenty-four hours. All she had to do was work out how to keep him away for over twenty-four hours. Somewhere public. Where his presence would be noticed – and maybe videoed for evidence. Then she'd have the ammunition she needed to remove his name from the deed. The house and land would be hers alone.

Perfect.

Maybe that should have been her mistletoe wish this Christmas instead of some lame idea about being part of a family.

But if she scammed him out of the bequest, he would lose this chance of sharing the holiday season with his daughter. And then there'd be another daughter without her beloved parent at Christmas. A memory rose of how he had glanced over to his car when they'd been helping that old man fix his tyre. Skye had been hanging half out of the side window; her eyes glued to her father. Sara had gained the impression there was a strong bond between Darim and his only child.

Her tummy churned and nausea rose. She dropped

the folder. She didn't want to be that woman anymore – one who ignored others' needs and the rules to satisfy her own desires. Turning her back on the folder, she snatched up her coffee and marched outside.

She found Darim already settled at the outdoor table which they had placed beneath a shady tree; one in a grove of twelve that after Darim had mown the grass, made an inviting setting. Three gaily striped hammocks now hung from the lowest branches of some of the trees. Perfect for lolling on during the hottest part of the day or for star gazing. Yesterday, Sara had planted some red and white geranium cuttings, and if they took would add splashes of bright colour and make the place look more … inviting.

Sliding onto the bench opposite, she pulled a plate towards her with one hand as she enjoyed her first caffeine hit of the day.

"I've been thinking about that bike ride." Darim munched on a crispy slice of bacon for a second before continuing.

Another thing she'd noticed – and liked – he never ate with his mouth open.

She stared pensively into her mug and nibbled on her lower lip. This constant focus on him had to stop.

"A bike would be the perfect Christmas gift for Skye. She'd be able to ride into town and visit her cousins. Gives her a bit of independence." He wagged his fork in the air. "I asked your friend, Ms. Lette, if she minded if more people came along, and she was fine with the idea. Us, my sister and her kids."

That crafty old witch was definitely not her friend. But … an ally - maybe. "What about school?"

"It's almost the end of term. I can't see it being a problem with Fatima."

"I don't believe I know your sister and her family."

"She moved here a few years ago with her mother-in-law and two daughters after her husband died of a stroke. She's my half-sister actually and two years older than me. We were quite close when we were young. Her mother who was a refugee from Syria died not long after she was born, and our father married my mother about a year later. She's the main reason why I'd like to settle in the area."

"Fatima. I think I may have seen her around town. Would she wear a hijab? Usually one in bright colours."

"That's sounds like her." Darim smiled. "She's a dentist and has a small practice in town. Neither of us sees much of my parents. They like to spend their retirement playing golf."

Sara examined his face. With his olive skin and dark eyes, she supposed he could also be Syrian. But what about his light brown hair? Some strands were bleached almost blond and there was the glint of silver, too. She gave into her curiosity. "Are you also Syrian?"

"My paternal grandfather was from Syria. The rest of our stock came from England and Scandinavia."

"Then not Muslim?"

A frown settled on his brow, and he actually drew back from the table. "No. That was a choice Fatima made when she was about eight. She decided to follow her mother's beliefs. Is that a problem for you?"

"Honestly, not in the least. My parents practiced different religions, which meant I grew up understanding a bit about both and a foot in both camps."

His frown disappeared as his rigid shoulders rounded. The sudden tension dissipated, and they smiled at each other. How odd to be so comfortable in his presence.

Darim started on his toast as Sara set down her mug and dug into her meal. She had to admit waking to a home-cooked breakfast – not to mention fresh coffee – was like a heaven-sent gift. As she ate, she thought about another day spent in his company. This time, however, instead of slogging away labouring on the property they would be taking a day off and in the company of others. Her pulse kicked up a gear as a lick of heady anticipation burned through her veins. Should she try to get out of the bike riding invitation? But that wasn't an option. Tessa and Dodge were counting on her being there; and considering the task they had charged her with there was no way she could refuse this late in the day. And besides, she really wanted to go. A swim in Ward's Gully would be wonderful in this heat.

She mopped up the last of her eggs with her remaining slice of toast. "You'll need a bike as well as finding one for your daughter."

"I know. Hence my early start to Armidale." He

reached over and his warm hand closed over the top of hers.

She looked up and met his earnest gaze.

"I want to thank you for helping me set this place up so Skye can visit. It means a lot to me."

His fingers tightened.

She wanted so much to turn her hand over and link her fingers with his. Instead, she froze and stared back as impassively as she could manage. "It's no big deal."

A frown flickered across his face. He released his grip. A coolness now lay between them. "It may not be to you, but it is to me. Whatever your motive, thank you." His words may have indicated gratitude, but there was no mistaking the ice in his voice.

Their truce was obviously over.

The problem was, she couldn't believe the strength of her disappointment. And how much it hurt to feel the distance between them widen.

She cared about his good opinion. Maybe she cared for more than that too.

Unable to speak, she fixed her gaze on her empty plate rather than look at him. Afraid of what he might see in her face.

If only she could push through her old fears and self-doubt. If only she could lower her walls but it seemed all she could do was push people away.

CHAPTER 7

Arms loose by his sides, back as straight as an arrow, Darim waited on the platform for the last train of the day to arrive from Sydney. Satisfaction sat like a cosy cloak on his shoulders. As if it had been one of his military operations, the day had gone exactly as planned. In the carpark, reposed his Land Rover with the used five metre caravan he'd purchased earlier that day attached to the towbar. Not as big as he had hoped, but at least it would provide alternate sleeping arrangements for Skye if she didn't wish to sleep in the house. It had a fabulous canvas awning off to one side, with shade cloth walls and a canvas floor that would provide another *'living'* area. Even better, he had a brand-new girl's bike wrapped and hidden in the rear of his vehicle under a tarp. He'd opted for a second-hand bike for himself, also hidden from view.

As soon as he picked up the fridge promised by his

sister, he'd be able to settle in and enjoy the holiday season with Skye. The past few days working alongside Sara had been quite an eye opener. Every time he thought about it, and if he wanted to be honest that was often, he found her company increasingly delightful. There was a serene if somewhat reserved air about her that drew him more enticingly than honey to a bee. Even if she wasn't as open as he would have liked, he was certain that given time they could become closer. A prospect that five days ago would have horrified him and sent him retreating to the hills.

Life was full of surprises.

A garbled voice came over the speakers. There was a horn blast and the train appeared. The few people waiting on the platform surged from where they sat on hard benches, wilting from the heat. Instantly the languid atmosphere was charged with energy.

With a belch of hot diesel-filled air, the train lurched to a stop. Doors slid open and passengers spilled out into the late afternoon.

"Dad!" shrieked a familiar voice.

And then his precious daughter was in his arms.

He hugged her tight, imprinting his memory with the bubble-gum scent of her shampoo, the tickle of her soft fair hair beneath his chin, and the eager way she clasped him around his neck. "You're taller," he finally managed to say when she wiggled out of his hold.

She danced around in front of him in sneakers glittering with orange and silver sequins, reaching for her wheeled unicorn suitcase while at the same time attempting to wrestle a bulging messenger bag over her shoulder. "I've been eating my Weet-Bix."

They grinned at each other, sharing a joke he'd been fond of saying when she was little.

His heart lurched.

Where had the years flown? Already, Skye showed signs of the young woman she would grow into; her previously chubby arms and legs had disappeared into long slim limbs. At least she had still retained his fair hair and brown eyes. The baby roundness of her cheeks had vanished revealing her mother's sculptured bones. And … *and … !!!*

"Is that a nose piercing?" His voice was way sharper and louder than he'd expected.

Skye's sunny smile morphed with warp speed into a sullen pout. "So what? Mum was okay with it."

Darim clamped his lips shut. Yep. His baby girl was gone. In her place was a young teenager who suddenly felt like a total stranger. After a second, he rolled his shoulders and scooped the wheeled case out of her hands.

Time to worry about their relationship later. Afterall that was what this holiday was about – a chance to cement a solid grounding between them that would never crumble under the weight of whatever the years ahead held. Hopefully only good things for his baby girl.

"Let's get on the road, hey?"

It appeared Skye was just as keen to put their brief discord behind them. She kept up a steady stream of chatter as they made their way to the car park, filling him in on her school year, how her bestie was no longer her bestie (although he knew from past experience that wouldn't be the case in a day or so's time), how mean one of her teacher's was and how awesome was another. He noticed though that she took care to mention very little about her mother and the new boyfriend, Antoine. She was in the middle of some long story about her netball team and their placing in the last season, when she stopped dead on the footpath.

"Is that our caravan?"

Hesitating as he scanned her shining face for any hint of Celeste's disdain, he finally admitted, "Affirmative. Got it today. What do you think?"

"I love it! And I'm totally crushing those sunflower curtains. I can't believe that you remembered yellow is my favourite colour." She clasped her hands together and blinked furiously over damp brown eyes. Then she launched herself onto his chest. "Thanks, Dad. You're the best."

Now was so not the time to admit the sunflower curtains were a complete fluke.

They got on the road and Darim headed south-west on the New England Highway. As the broiling sun slowly sunk over the horizon, his daughter enlivened the journey with her choice of music off her iPad while talking nineteen to the dozen. It was when they turned onto Halls Creek Road near Bendemeer that she broached the loaded subject he had yet to address in any detail.

"I can't believe you've got a house. Does it have a pool? Can I have a pony?" She bounced on the seat beside him.

"No pool, although there is a public swimming pool in town as well as a river and a creek." He sent her a sideways glance before switching on the headlights revealing the winding road ahead. Bushland and scrub grew thick and dark as the encroaching night deepened the shadows. He stashed his sunnies into a pocket on the driver's side door. "Not sure about the pony. I know zero about horses. But in the next couple of days, we'll have some llamas. They're Sara's."

"Llamas!" Skye's eyes grew round as she stared at him. Then … "Who's Sara?"

Darim shifted uncomfortably on the seat. This was the moment that had occupied his thoughts lately. How the devil to divulge the exact nature of their living situation? Tell it all with no embellishments. Get it done and dusted. "The thing is hon." Then out it came. The reminder of the chance meeting all those years ago with an old man and Sara. The bequest, although he brushed over the stipulations and how he only had shared ownership. He wound up by saying, "The house is quite small. There's only one room, although we've fixed up the small bathroom out back. You can either share a bunk bed with Sara or sleep in the van with me."

"Wow. That is so … Does Mum know about this?"

"She knows I've got a house, but not the part about the conditions and Sara's inclusion in the bequest."

Darim paused and switched to a lower gear as the road rose to a steep incline.

"Will I like her?"

"I think so. She seems an intelligent if rather reserved woman." Even he knew that wasn't what his daughter wanted to hear. He could feel her intense gaze fastened on his face. Despite exercising extreme control, he failed to stop the flush burning across his cheeks and neck.

"Dad. Come on. Is she pretty? What does she look like? Does she work? Does she like animals? Kids?"

Feeling as if he was stepping into a pit full of live and hungry man-eating crocodiles, he cleared his throat and mumbled, "Well. She's kinda okay I guess. She's got very dark eyes and black hair."

Hair so shiny he longed to run his fingers over the strands. Eyes so inky dark and mysterious, he longed to stare into them for …

There was a sudden grating crash and the Land Rover jolted sideways. Darim's idiotic musings smashed into smithereens.

"*Shit!* Hang on Skye." He wrestled with the steering wheel as the Land Rover shuddered and the mind-splitting noise continued. The vehicle veered sharply to the right, careening into the other lane.

Skye screamed but there was no time to comfort her.

Sweat pooled under Darim's armpits as he simultaneously attempted to slow their speed by working through the gears and gently easing down on the brakes, while guiding them back onto the right side of the road.

The Land Rover rocked and swayed. A quick glance in the rear vision mirror showed the shadowy lump of the van they towed, doing the same as they swerved from one lane to the other. If it rocked too far in one direction, the van could well over balance altogether and send both vehicles into a roll that could prove disastrous.

Another look in all directions. They were hemmed in on both sides by dense bush and closely packed trees. And who knew what the contours of the land was like once past those first stand of trees. It could be more bush or a steep drop.

With one last massive lurch the Land Rover righted. Darim applied more pressure on the brakes and, finally, the vehicles came to a juddering halt.

"Are you okay?" He snicked off his seat belt and reached for Skye.

However, she was already undoing her own belt and sent him a shaky smile. "All good, Dad. What happened?"

Running a hand over his face, he shook his head. "No idea. But I bet it has something to do with the van. Maybe we blew a tyre or even two." He pulled a torch out of the glove box. "Stay here and keep your mobile on while I check it out. Any reception?"

"No bars," Skye said glumly, holding her phone up for him to see.

After giving her shoulder a gentle squeeze, Darim

pushed open his door and stepped out into the night. He flicked on the torch and began a careful sweep; first of the Land Rover then finding nothing obvious, moved to the towbar and the front of the caravan.

"Damn." Worse than a blown tyre. One of the metal struts of the A-frame that linked the chassis to the towing hitch, had split and was dragging on the ground. He bent down and ran his hands along the metal. Powdery residue coated his fingers. A closer inspection revealed a dodgy paint job had been applied to cover up the rusted metal. There could be rust all throughout the chassis. Lowering himself to the stony ground, he wriggled on his back under the van and shone the torch around. The axle had snapped into two, with the larger piece of metal now reposing in the dirt. They needed a tow truck.

A blue light flickered about. "Did you find the problem?" came Skye's voice.

"Damnit, Skye. I told you to wait in the car."

"It's dark out here, Dad. I didn't want to be alone."

"Yeah, okay, I understand. Sorry, hon. Move out of the way while I get myself out." He shuffled and slithered until he was able to stand. A thorough shine of the torch in all directions revealed nothing but an empty road in both directions surrounded by trees and yet more trees. No house lights. No signs of any oncoming vehicles. They were on their own.

"Can you fix it?"

"That's a negative." He explained about the rust and broken axle. "My fault, I obviously didn't do a thorough inspection. Guess I was taken in by the seller being who I thought was a nice single mother." He sighed and looked around again. "I can't see any properties where we can ask for help. Let's get back into the car. I'm going to drive the car and the van further away from the road. There's a bit of a clearing a few metres ahead where we can park."

As they walked back to the Land Rover, he slung an arm around his daughter and hugged her close. "We've got two options. Stay here and hope that someone comes along, and we can flag them down. The other option is we leave the van and drive on until we get a phone connection. I'm leaning towards the latter option."

"I don't want to stay here, Dad." Shivering she snuggled up against him.

He popped a kiss on her forehead before opening the passenger door and shooing her inside. "That's settled then. We'll move the caravan away from the road, then go find help."

As he closed the door, he remembered one of the stipulations of the bequest; no party to be away from the property for longer than twenty-four hours. He checked his watch. Fifteen past eighteen hundred hours. No sweat. He could still make it back well within the time limit.

Ten minutes later and the dark outline of the caravan was disappearing in the rear. The former gaiety inside the cabin had vanished. Skye sat huddled in the corner and clutching her mobile to her chest.

Not the best start to what he hoped would be a turning point in their relationship. But as every good soldier knew, campaigns were fluid, always changing, and if you wanted to win you had to be prepared to re-group and re-evaluate at every eventuality.

IT WAS after midnight when they finally arrived at the shack.

Darim took a moment to shake off his fatigue and drink in the sight of the welcoming lights flowing from the window and open door. Before he could rouse Skye awake, a figure burst onto the verandah and ran across the grass.

"What happened?" yelled Sara. She reached the Land Rover and wrenched open the door. The interior light switched on revealing her tense features. "It's been hours!"

"Worried about me, were you?" He ran his knuckles down her pale cheek and felt her quiver at his touch. What would it be like to have her throw her arms around him and hold him tight?

Eyes flitting past him to rest on Skye, she muttered, "Don't be ridiculous. I was thinking about your daughter."

"Seriously, we're fine. Although I can't say the same about the van." He sighed and entertained the insane idea of folding her into his arms and drinking in her sweet scent. "It's a long story."

Sara's nose wrinkled. "I can smell McDonalds." She

smiled and it was as if everything was right in his world once more.

"That was dinner," he admitted wryly then leaning over, he gently touched Skye's wrist. "Come on, hon. We're home."

Giving a massive yawn, Skye blinked then stared at Sara before looking out the windscreen and frowning. "The house doesn't look very big."

Sara laughed. "It's small but cosy. Come inside and relax while I make you a hot chocolate."

"Really?" The doubt left his daughter's face as her eyes lit up.

Chocolate.

The magic word which worked every time.

They trooped inside the house, with Darim pulling the suitcase and Sara taking the messenger bag off Skye. Under the brutal glare of the single light bulb, the furniture looked shabby despite the yellow and white checked throw rug adorning the grey sofa and the orange butterfly doona on the bunks. A pedestal fan blasted warm air in their faces, only marginally cooler than the air outside. Darim stuffed his hands in his pockets. Would Skye turn up her nose? How much of her mother's snobby attitude had rubbed off on her?

"I claim the top bunk!" She scampered across the room and hauled herself onto the bed. Trailing a hand over the doona, she grinned. "My favourite colours."

"Same. I'm a yellow and orange kind of girl," said Sara.

They shared a smile.

And to Darim it was as if some kind of secret understanding passed between them. That hard knot in his gut he hadn't realised he'd been carrying, dissolved.

"Darim, why don't you sit down and tell me all about your day." Sara moved to the kitchenette and began to prepare their drinks.

He obeyed without a murmur which made his daughter giggle, and as she hugged a pillow and watched with bright eyes, he relayed the news about the caravan. "The tow company should deliver the van late tomorrow afternoon."

Sara handed a mug to Skye then another to him. Picking up another mug, she perched on a stool and blew on the hot contents. "It's a shame this happened on the first day of your holidays, Skye. Did your father mention there's a Christmas tree to erect and decorate?"

"No! Where is it?"

Sara indicated the box on the floor and Skye immediately climbed down the top bunk and raced over. "Also did he tell you about what we're doing tomorrow?"

Darim's eyebrows shot skywards. The last time they had discussed the bike ride, Sara had attempted to dissuade him from attending. Now the sweet smile on her lips made him think that she was looking forward to his presence. "Not yet. Why don't you tell her while I get something from the car?"

She nodded, obviously knowing exactly what he was up to and began to speak. Trying to act as if he wasn't rushing, Darim put down his mug and disappeared out the door.

Sara was in the middle of describing the swimming hole when he poked his head around the corner.

He was just in time to hear his daughter's wailing response. "I can't go. I don't have a bike!"

Then he pushed the clumsily wrapped girl's bike into the room. "Happy Christmas, sweetheart."

Giving a loud squeal, Skye leapt from where she was surrounded by baubles and tinsel and seemed to fly across the room. She flung her arms around his neck. Squeezed. Then danced around the bike, oohing and aahing. "Can I unwrap it now?"

"Sure." He handed it over and went to stand beside Sara.

Together they watched Skye peel off the Christmas paper before sitting astride the bike and ringing the bell. "It's awesome, Dad. Thank you." She hesitated then added shyly, "Thanks, Sara."

Although Sara had had nothing to do with his purchase, it suddenly struck Darim that the way they were gathered around was exactly like a family.

And he was where he was meant to be.

CHAPTER 8

For the umpteenth time, Sara checked the package reposing in the basket at the front of her bike. No problems there. Smiling, she pushed hard on the peddles as she followed the group of riders along the bumpy track that lead to a popular swimming hole in Bindarra Creek. The intense heat was oppressive under the full glare of the harsh morning sun, leaving her skin prickling with sweat. The relief promised by shady trees and cool water propelled her onwards.

On the left was a large grazing property with a country house and assorted barns half hidden behind a grove of shady trees. Dense bushland edged its boundaries. On the right, there were four smaller farm allotments with old homes in various stages of disrepair. No one appeared to be home as she rode by apart from a flock of chickens pecking along the rutted drive of the third farm. As she came closer to the fourth, she noticed a car parked in the drive. A woman stood with her back to them apparently looking at the front porch. She looked over her shoulder as her dog jumped to his feet and barked. But she placed a soothing hand on his head, and he quietened. Sara waved and the woman waved back with a friendly smile on her face.

"That must be the grinch's American lady!" called Fatima's eldest daughter Uri from further ahead.

The younger girls waved madly and called out *'cooee'* and *'welcome to Oz'*.

Sara laughed. Seriously? Bindarra Creek had their very own grinch?

Finally, they were approaching the last property on the right which had been abandoned many years ago and left to return to its natural form. The fences bordering the overgrown paddocks were little more than bales of tangled wire and broken posts. Saplings and shrubs of wild rosemary, bottlebrush and grevilleas grew unchecked. A mob of kangaroos, some dozing beneath the shade of a tall eucalypt tree and some grazing on tufts of grass, stared with inquisitive eyes at the parade of noisy people. Overhead, the sky was a brilliant blue and a heat haze shimmered in the distance.

She couldn't believe how happy and how humble she felt that Tessa had included her in the bike ride on such a special day. It was if she had turned a corner in her life and her relationships with others. It was if she was now part of something bigger than herself. And that she was truly no longer alone.

It had been a bit of a scramble to retrieve the promised package for Tessa and Dodge then make it to where everyone was meeting on the abandoned farm lot at the end of Diggers Lane. She'd parked her Holden ute on the drive leading into Abby and Roman's acreage, hefted her bike from the back and ridden along Bindarra Creek Road until she came to the turn off. It had been far too hot for her to peddle all the way from her new home out on River Road – not with the little charge under her protection. She rather suspected quite a few others would be glad of a lift back to town by the end of the day. It was surprising how many people and bikes you could fit in a ute's tray.

She'd left earlier than Darim and Skye, wanting to time her arrival so she could ride at the end of the pack. That suited her just fine as she wasn't a particularly proficient bike rider and if she was anywhere near the front she'd probably slow people down. Even the elderly couple wobbling down the road on a tandem were better riders than her.

Grinning, she tugged the baseball hat she wore under her helmet a tad lower over her forehead and slowed as she neared the broken gate to the old farm. She'd told Darim she had to pick up the birthday gift, and he gave her a nod as she lingered well away from everyone especially the lady of the day.

Thankfully Ms. Edwina Lette was surrounded by her closest friends and sometimes partners in crime; Pamela Brown, Beatrix and Maki Fukuka, and the Millers who were the couple astride the tandem bike.

Tessa gave Sara a wave. Her bike had one of those kiddie trailers attached with her youngest daughter, Tilly sitting inside. Her eldest daughter Kaylee rode her own bike and seemed to be making friends with Skye and Skye's two cousins, Ousa and Uri.

Sara fought back a giggle at the sight of a sweating Dodge who was manning the bicycle pulling a rickshaw where Edwina perched grinning gleefully and calling out *'Mush! Mush!'* every so often.

Where on earth he had sourced a rickshaw from, she had no idea. But it certainly was an effective and fun way to dissuade their grandmother from insisting she ride a bike. After her narrow escape a few months ago, the elderly lady was under orders not to pursue any strenuous exercises for some time.

Everyone staggered to a stop. Skye laughingly snapped off a shot of the rickshaw on her mobile then showed it to the other young girls. Sara wasn't aware that Darim had circled back until he spoke.

"That rickshaw is quite something."

"I rather think it was Tessa's idea. Since she married Dodge, she's come up with quite a few innovative suggestions to revitalise the town."

Ms. Lette poked a hand from the side of the rickshaw and gave a languid movement as if she was a queen bestowing a knighthood.

Darim laughed and touched Sara's arm. "I want you to meet my sister. Fatima, this is Sara Pyeon, the woman who has joint ownership of the property with me."

"Pleased to meet you." Smiling, Sara extended her hand, hoping it wasn't too damp and sticky.

Fatima Maloof was a forty-something woman with strong features in a round good-humoured face, and with her younger brother's rich-brown eyes. A candy-pink and white hijab covered her hair. She wore white three-quarter pants and a thin long-sleeve pink shirt. Like her brother, she also had a wicker basket strapped to the rear of her bicycle. "I'm so glad to meet you, Sara. Congratulations on the bequest. It's a wonderful opportunity for both of you. I can't tell you how excited I am that my little brother will be living so close to us." She beckoned a fifty-odd man with thick silver hair and a shiny, perspiring face to step forward. "Do you know Ernest Callen?"

Sara nodded to the older man. "We've met. I was on the same search team as you when Ms. Lette went missing last July."

"I remember." A flush deepened the reddish hue of his skin and his gaze dropped as if he was ashamed to meet her eyes.

She wasn't surprised by his reaction although his involvement in Ms. Lette's kidnapping several months ago had been tenuous to say the least. Because on one level he *was* culpable for the elderly lady and a teenage boy's traumatic experiences. It was through his actions a would-be killer had come to town. But who was she to judge? She knew all about bad choices. And in the end, he had risked his own life to save others.

"It's good to see you again, Mr. Callen."

His head rose and a shy smile twisted his lips. "Ernest, please."

"If everyone's had some water and a rest, let's move on!" called Tessa as she handed her youngest, Tilly, a bottle of juice.

"Put some effort into it, boy. I want a swim and a taste of my birthday cake before the sun sets!" Ms. Lette produced a riding crop and brought it down with a loud snap against the side of the rickshaw.

The younger girls squealed, while everyone else laughed and mounted their bikes.

Dodge saluted. "Yes, ma'am!"

A rustle came from inside Sara's basket, no doubt roused by all the noise. She slid a calming hand inside as she set off again. This time, Darim rode alongside her.

"I can make a good guess as to what you have in that basket." He grinned. Apart from a couple of beads of sweat adorning his upper lip, he showed no signs of puffing or struggle to keep the wheels turning. Especially given that he and Skye had ridden all the way from the shack which was a lot further than the distance travelled for those who lived in town. He certainly was fit.

As for Sara, her scalp was itchy beneath her helmet and her clothes sticking uncomfortably to her flesh. At least her level of fitness was on a par with his; it was only the heat she struggled with. Hoping he didn't spot her lingering glance on his muscled forearms, she merely shushed him with a quick finger to her mouth.

Her heart stuttered as his gaze followed and he swallowed. It seemed he wasn't as composed as he always made out to be. Although it was hard to be sure he felt the same dangerous attraction since sunglasses shielded his eyes.

A girl could hope.

It wasn't long before the narrow track winding through the scrub and bush emerged onto the banks of Bindarra Creek. Rolling her shoulders, Sara hopped off her bike and kicked down the stand. Everyone else was milling about, grabbing their gear off their bikes or, in the case of the kids, heading straight for the water's edge.

"What a perfect spot." Darim approached her, a picnic basket in his hands.

Sara glanced around, absorbing the almost yen tranquility of the creek's flow, the gentle sigh of shifting willow tree branches and the dappled sunlight tiptoeing over the boulders lining the banks. A kookaburra burst forth with his familiar warble. Swallows weaved in and out around the trees. A willy wagtail strutted his stuff on a nearby branch while butterflies and dragonflies flittered over the water's surface. Ducks paddled in the shallows. With a few disgruntled quacks they moved further downstream. There was nothing to remind anyone of the tense events that had been played out several months ago when Edwina's and a young boy's lives had been at stake.

In the clearing on the other side of the creek, a long trestle table had been set up together with several camp chairs. Newlyweds Natalie and Troy Davidson waved heartily from where they stood in the shade next to the quads they must have ridden to get to the gully. They had been charged with setting up for the celebration. By the looks of the two eskies bulging with cold drinks and the number of cakes and plates crammed onto the table, they had done an excellent job. Colourful paper flowers had been strung together with crystal beads and hung from the tree spreading its branches above the table.

Sara waited beside her bike with Darim, until Tessa had popped Tilly out of the bike trailer and strolled over.

"All good?"

"I think so." After unsnapping the straps securing the basket to her handlebars, Sara offered her the package.

Kaylee rushed forward, eyes shining. "Mum! Mum! Can I do it, please?"

"No. Me!" squealed Tilly tugging on her mother's pant leg.

Eyebrows raised, Tessa sent Dodge a questioning look.

In the middle of helping his grandmother out of the rickshaw – despite her hand slapping and exclamations that she required no such help – he smiled and nodded.

It struck Sara how much of a team this young couple were – they were a complete unit. Standing shoulder to shoulder. Their mutual respect and love were truly something to behold; and while Sara liked them both very much, wistfulness stabbed deep. She blinked away sudden moisture. What would it be like to have that kind of relationship?

"I'm not in my dotage yet, Dodge. Now get out of my way while I cross the creek. That birthday cake is calling me." With a huff and a toss of her long grey hair, Edwina hitched the hem of the scarlet and lime-green filmy dress she wore and flitted across the boulders with the grace and surety of a teenager.

"Damnit, Gran!" Her grandson ran after her, arms outstretched as if ready to catch her should she fall.

"You can both give the gift to Gran. But Kaylee will carry it across the creek." Snatching Tilly up into her arms, Tessa picked her away from one slippery boulder to the next until she reached the other side. She ensured she was blocking the view of Kaylee, and no doubt the basket her daughter was carrying.

Accompanied by squeals and gasps, everyone else quickly scrambled over. No one wanted to miss the main event.

"Sit here, Gran." Dodge all but pushed Edwina into a camp chair. He then clapped Troy on the shoulder saying, "Thanks, mate. Everything looks fantastic."

Troy laughed. "No worries. Natalie did most of the work. I was just the labourer."

"Well? What are you all waiting for?" Edwina's eyes fastened on Kaylee and the basket with a hungry gleam.

"Nothing gets past you, Gran," Dodge chuckled.

"I need my smokes." She began to slap at her dress.

Her best friend, Pamela Brown, scowled. "Not now, Edwina."

Dodge moved to stand beside his wife who placed Tilly onto the ground. Kaylee took her sister's hand, and they moved forward together. Clearing his throat, Dodge said in a husky voice, "This is for you."

Kaylee laid the basket on Edwina's lap while Tilly leaned close to her side.

Everyone crowded forward. No one spoke as if they all held their breaths. As for Sara, she watched with a lump in her throat, knowing how bitter-sweet this moment was for the old lady and her family.

Edwina opened the lid. Sucked in her breath. She hesitated; her hands poised above the open basket. Then she dived inside and brought out a squirming, black and tan puppy with super long floppy ears. He had a small slash of white down his chest and his tail was wagging overtime.

Kaylee took the basket away and slipped an arm around Edwina's shoulders.

Dodge stepped forward to place a gentle kiss on the top of her grey head. "We all miss Rufus, and he can never be replaced. He was our best mate, but he was your best mate most of all. What do you say, Granny? Is it okay to add another member to our family?"

"He's perfect." A few tears slipped from her eyes and slid down her wrinkled cheeks. "Yes. Oh, yes." With a grin beaming from ear to ear, Edwina settled the dashhound puppy on her lap. "I'm going to call him, Boris."

"Boris! Ick." Kaylee pulled a face.

Edwina winked. "I knew a Boris once."

"Not again!" Pamela threw her hands in the air and her sister, Beatrix giggled.

Kaylee planted a kiss on the side of her grandmother's face. "Oh, in that case, I love the name Boris. Happy birthday, Granny."

"Thank you, child."

Tilly demanded, "I want to hold him."

"You can sit on my lap but you have to be gentle. He's only a baby." Gran lifted the puppy in the air as Tilly slid over her knees. "Now, where's my cake?"

People began to drift away. The vicar, Florrie Miller steered her husband, Jonas, over to a camp chair and got him settled with an iced tea. Beatrix and Maki pulled out a couple of bottles of their home-made organic wine and some plastic cups. The kids reefed off their outer clothes and headed to the creek. Tessa located a pair of floaties for Tilly and patiently waited beside Edwina while Tilly petted the pup.

Dodge ordered, "No jumping or diving, you lot. Kaylee, that means you."

"Yes, Dad." Kaylee whispered something to Skye, and they giggled as they stepped into the water with Ousa and Uri.

The girls shrieked and called out varying versions of, "Oooh, its cold!"

"I'll keep an eye on them." Darim placed his picnic basket near the table and moved over to the edge to stand sentry. "Don't go out into the middle, Skye. The current is still running fast after that last storm."

"Seriously, Dad? I'm a junior lifesaver at Bondi Beach."

Smiling as father and daughter continued to argue, Sara removed the jumbo-sized Tupperware container of fruit salad and a tub of Greek yoghurt then added both to the groaning table. She chucked off her clothes, laying them neatly in a pile before treading carefully over the bindi covered ground.

"Are you coming in?" she asked Darim who stood arms folded and frowning at the water's edge.

His eyes lit up as they examined her modest emerald-green swimsuit, and a wolfish smile curled his lips. "Sweetheart, one day and soon; we're going swimming. Alone."

"Is that a promise – or a challenge?" She popped a hand on one hip and added with no trace of a smile on her face and a hard thump of her heart, "Because either way, I can handle anything you care to dish out."

"I know. That's what I'm counting on." Sneaking an arm about her waist, he tugged her close and his lips grazed her temple.

For several pulse pounding, tummy churning seconds, she stood tense and stiff uncertain how to react. She was acutely aware of his daughter's widened eyes.

Tessa whispered with a wide grin, as she walked past with Tilly, "Gran is never wrong."

But her words only dimly registered.

As Sara sucked in a shaky breath, all she was aware of and all she could feel was Darim's searing male heat branding her heart forever. What she longed for more than anything was to turn into his embrace and kiss him. To taste his lips on hers.

Doubt held her back.

But if she didn't tell him about her past, he could eventually hear about it from someone else.

Then what kind of a relationship would they have? Him knowing she'd kept such a dark secret from him. Her racked with guilt because she hadn't trusted him.

That wasn't the life she wanted them to share.

He deserved the truth.

Whether he could ever understand and forgive, however, was a black cloud that sucked the life from her soul.

And kept her rigid in his arms.

CHAPTER 9

Darim felt distinctly grouchy when he stalked inside the shack the following morning after rapping on the door and been given the okay to enter. A decent sleep had eluded him. Instead, he had spent the majority of the night plotting and wondering how to dismantle Sara's defenses. It seemed she was determined to keep him at arm's length, despite the mutual attraction that amplified by the hour. There had been a moment at the rock pool, when he'd honestly thought she had been about to kiss him. But she'd beat a hasty retreat. Worse, he'd spotted a deep sadness in the darkness of her eyes. Unable to do anything to erase it had burned like a cauterised wound all night long. It wasn't in him to sit on the sidelines when someone was in need. He was a fixer of problems - a protector.

Unfortunately, Sara wasn't having any of it or him.

That vague idea he'd had of forcing her out of their

joint ownership had vanished. What he wanted now was a more intimate partnership.

Apparently, not only was Sara not listening but so was the universe. Maybe it was time he tried a mistletoe wish.

His gaze sought and found her the instant he set foot over the threshold. She was dressed in faded jeans and a long sleeve white tee. Her shiny black hair was pulled back from her face in a low ponytail. But it was her complexion that held him still; normally a light golden honey shade, she was pale and there were smudges beneath her eyes.

She looked up from where she was folding a blanket.

And stiffened.

Damnit. He couldn't read a thing from her impassive expression.

"What's llama day?" Skye stabbed a finger on the yellow sticky note attached to the wall behind the camp stove. "Is this something to do with the llamas you were talking about Dad?"

He grunted an affirmative.

"Cool."

Laying the blanket neatly on the couch, Sara then moved over to the stove and handed him his coffee. "You sound like you need this."

"Sorry. Rough night." He took the mug and nodded his thanks.

"Couldn't sleep?" she asked.

"My mind wouldn't shut down."

"Same." Lowering her voice, she bit her lip. "Have you had a chance to get another solicitor's opinion about the bequest and all those conditions?"

"I emailed my lawyers a copy a couple of days ago. However, what with Christmas and their shut down period they couldn't give an indication of when they could get back to me."

"Pity."

What the devil was she thinking?

He took a sip of his bitter brew then said, "Look. About our arrangement here – you know how important it is to me, but what about yourself? You've never told me what's at stake here for you."

"Boring," sang out Skye from where she'd perched on the stool. "I want to know about the llamas."

The tension straining between him and Sara dissipated when she smiled.

"Today, we're moving my llamas from a paddock a few clicks out of town to here."

"Why do you have llamas? Are they your pets or something?"

Sara shook her head as she moved to the kitchenette and began to pour cereal into a bowl. She added a splash of long-life milk and offered it to Skye. "Not pets, although they are really cute." She flicked Darim a quick glance before replacing the containers in the cupboard. "My goal is to run my own business which is why I need land. The house doesn't really faze me. I could camp in a tent if I really had to."

Skye crunched on her cereal then waved her spoon

in the air. "I don't know anyone who has a llama. This is way cool. Go on please, Sara. How many llamas do you have?"

"I only have three at the moment. Two young females and one male. By the way, as they are only a few months old, they are called crias. My intention is to build up a herd and make hand-woven, dyed rugs, wall hangings, that kind of thing from their wool. They produce a strong soft low-micron wool that is lanolin free and also come in a wide range of natural colours. So I may not dye all of the products I want to make. Once I have a decent size herd, I'll probably sell some of the wool direct to knitters and spinners as well. I may also make hats and jackets from their fleece."

"You'll need a decent website, one with shopping facilities," Darim advised.

"Agreed. Abby and Roman's eldest son Drew is a whizz with computers. He's just finished a website for Troy Davidson's new venture. Troy's a newbie in town. He arrived last July; apparently he's related to Ms. Lette and her family." She tilted her head and considered him. "He's ex-Army and has set up a hang-gliding business out in the Akuna National Park."

"I believe I met him at a recent local business gathering when we discussed a few of our military training initiatives we intend to run in the area. We were investigating the impact, if any, these activities may have on the town in general. I also wanted to see whether it was feasible to incorporate hang-gliding into the training."

Skye set her empty bowl down in the sink and

rinsed it. "Dad. No army talk, okay? Llamas are way more interesting."

He laughed and ruffled her hair as she passed.

"Awwww, seriously? Now I need to fix my hair again."

"It doesn't need fixing. You're perfect as you are."

"You are so lame." His daughter rolled her eyes, but her grin was wide erasing any sting in her words. "Sara, about your llamas. What are their names?"

"I haven't called them anything yet," she admitted.

"No way! Ooooh, can I name one please?" Skye placed her hands beneath her chin and widened her eyes.

Sara looked at her, a smile tugging at her lips then turned to Darim. "One word. Precocious."

"She was born that way." He grinned.

"I bet," Sara said in a dry voice. "Yes, you can name one of them."

"This is so cool. Wait until I tell my bestie. She's going to be green!" So saying, Skye scampered over to the dresser and yanked open a drawer. She tossed a pair of socks onto the bed. "Are you two ready yet?"

"I guess it's time to go." Darim raised his eyebrows.

"I'll get my hat."

He caught Sara by the hand as she went to brush past. "Is this what you meant about starting again? Your new business with the llamas, I mean."

She waited a beat. The tip of her tongue darted out and ran over her lower lip.

Clenching his jaw, he battled the need to drag her

into his arms and kiss her until she divulged what was eating away at her.

The expression in her eyes however cooled his heated blood in an instant. They were hollowed out, as if the laughter of a few moments ago had never been.

"When my parents died not that long ago, there was nothing left but debts. I had to sell the little that we owned to cover all the costs. I'd already lost my job, so I was left with nothing but a few clothes and a couple of momentoes. About two to three years ago, I came to Bindarra Creek hoping for a fresh start. Unfortunately, full-time work has been impossible to find. I worked for Dodge for a while, but he could only give me a few hours here and there. My job at the hospital is only casual and the bank has so far refused to approve my loan application. That's why this place is important to me. Setting up my own business is everything. I won't fail. Not again."

The way she chose her words with care warned there was more behind her reasons of why she had to start over. He had no idea what haunted her, but whatever it was, it was serious. Deep in thought, he closed the door behind Sara and Skye.

If anyone deserved a chance to start over, it was Sara.

KNEES STILL TREMBLING after *that* conversation, Sara slipped a rope halter over the biggest llama and tightened the slip knot. They had driven to Grady Ferguson's farm in Darim's Land Rover after he insisted it was far too hot to consider walking back with the animals. When they had arrived, Grady had offered the use of his horse float to ferry the llamas home. An offer, Sara had gratefully accepted.

Clicking softly with her tongue, she began to lead the male towards the gate. The two young females ambled forward along with a couple of donkeys. A goat with a long straggling beard blinked with curious eyes then went back to munching on grass. Under the shade of three small trees, reposed another donkey, four sheep and a very old and gaunt horse.

Grady and Opal, bless them, were obviously still agisting Maki's rescue animals. Her acquaintance with that young couple was sufficient for her to suspect they didn't charge him either. As it was, she had had difficulty in forcing them to accept a meagre payment for the use of this paddock for her llamas. In the end, she had told them her situation was different from Maki's – hers was business. Whilst his was a charity.

As she approached the gate, Darim opened it. One hand holding back the contraption of barbed wire and steel posts, he looked around her at the following animals. "Hold on. You've snagged a couple of hangers-ons."

"Dad, I'd love a donkey," Skye pleaded from where she waited beside the horse float. Dancing from one foot to the other, she almost vibrated with excitement.

Darim grinned. "I thought you wanted a pony?"

"I want a donkey *and* a pony. *And* a llama."

"The list is growing." Sara laughed as she urged the male cria to take a few more steps. He baulked at the bottom of the ramp leading into the horse float, flinging his head up and showing the whites of his eyes.

She crooned, "It's okay, boy. You're safe. No one is going to hurt you."

Ears twitching madly, the two females crowded behind him, jostling. Their soft leather pads stamping softly over twigs and fallen leaves.

"What's that noise?" Skye's eyes rounded as she backed away from the animals.

"It's the llamas. They're humming. It's one of the ways they communicate." Sara gently slid her hand over the male llama's nose. The action seemed to calm him. With one last snorting hum, he lowered his head and regarded the open horse float then looked at her. She ran her hand along his neck and over the curves of his back, then applied a little pressure on his rear end. With cautious steps, he minced into the float where she tied the end of his halter rope to the bar.

The two females trotted up with no problems. It only took a few more minutes and Sara had their halters on as well and then they were also secured. She emerged from the float to find Darim had fixed the gate into place as well as shooed the donkeys back into the paddock. She went to the Land Rover and rummaged inside her backpack returning with bunches of carrots in her hands. "I brought these especially to give to the other animals. Would you like to feed them, Skye?"

"Oh, yes please." The young girl took a handful and skipped to the fence where she waved a carrot in front of one of the donkeys. "Come on. Here's your dinner."

After they had fed the animals, they climbed into the Land Rover and Darim drove back to the property. There Sara asked Skye if she'd like to help, much to her delight. It wasn't long before all three llamas were out of the float and in the small corral Darim had erected in the paddock closest to the house.

"This is the best fun," Skye said as she carefully ran a brush down the dark brown female's leg. "How about we call this one Cher?"

Sara grinned as she removed the halter from the male. "I like it. Then this has to be Sonny. What about the other cria?"

Skye stopped brushing and frowned as she looked at the cream-coloured llama. "I'm not sure."

"I reckon Frankie is a good name." Resting his arms along the top rail, Darim smiled.

"Frankie it is," said Sara.

Uttering an ear-splitting scream, Skye pointed towards the grass. "I saw a snake!"

Darim hissed in a sharp breath. "Don't move. Stay exactly where you are. Sara, you're closer. Can you see anything? I can't."

Craning her neck and wishing she was five inches taller, Sara examined the ground near the patch of grass growing around the fence post. "It's okay. It's only a goanna. Come a little closer, Skye, and I'll show you." She beckoned the young girl forward.

After a glance at her father who nodded, Skye moved over to stand beside her.

"I think it's a lace monitor. Look how fat he is," Sara said as Darim joined them.

"Oh, there he goes."

With a flick of his tail the lizard scurried over the ground and up the nearest tree to disappear amongst the branches.

"That was cool. I've never seen a goanna in the wild before."

Darim slung an arm around his daughter and hugged her. "Well done for not moving, hon."

Smiling, she squirmed out of his hold and returned to brushing Sonny.

"I'll put those hay bales in the shed." He strode off to where a haphazard pile of bales had been stacked outside the rickety tin shed.

"I'll give your father a hand." Feeling guilty about the amount of work she'd piled onto his shoulders, Sara hurried after him. These were her animals after all; her responsibility. She should be the one building shelters and storing their feed. She went to heave up a bale but toppled onto her butt in the dirt.

Laughing, she picked herself up.

Darim grinned. "I'm all over this, Sara."

"At least let me get the door." She stomped over and unlatched the shed door, holding it open as it had a tendency to swing shut and slice into any unsuspecting person's ankle.

"Skye is loving all this – thank you so much for inviting us along today." He walked past, forearms bulging from the bale he carried.

"It would have taken me forever on my own, so your company was most welcome. Besides, I enjoyed it."

Darim winked at her, his gaze sweeping her from head to foot. "So did I. That swim and bike ride was a lot of fun too. I like being around you, Sara, and so does Skye."

Her face heated at the loaded look he gave her. She curled her fingers tighter over the door, fighting the flutter of desire and excitement turning her belly to water. "If you'd like more fun, there's the Christmas Carols on the 17th. Its being held in the showgrounds."

"Are you asking me out on a date?"

She shuffled her feet. "Hardly. It's a family do."

"Then we'll go together. You. Me. Skye."

His decisive voice took her breath away. Was he implying they were … a family?

"Any guest singers?"

Head still whirling, Sara gave a breathless chuckle. "Sorry. You'll have to make do with the locals. Some have half-way decent voices; some are very enthusiastic which kinda says it all. The evening will start off with school kids, a few solo acts etc."

"Sounds great. We'll organise a picnic dinner."

"There'll be a barbeque for those who want something hot as well as a coffee van."

"Even better." Darim moved in and out of the shed, stacking the bales of hay one on top of the other. When he'd finished, he stepped back slapping strands off his hands and jeans.

"Thanks for your help, today," Sara said as she tried to pretend she wasn't fascinated by the sight of him moving bales around as if they weighed little more than a cushion.

"It's all good, Sara. We make a good team." He smiled and her heart almost seized at the warmth and … something else that glowed hot and deep in his dark eyes. "I need to talk to you."

He stepped forward and captured one of her hands. "I've done a lot of serious thinking lately, Sara, and what you told me this morning has cemented my decision. I intend to forfeit my claim on the property."

"What!" She could feel her jaw drop at his revelation.

"It's quite simple really. You need this place to generate an income for yourself while I already have a job and some money in the bank. Although, child support takes quite a whack out of it, not that I begrudge it. Skye's my daughter. I want her to be secure and have a good education. I should be able to get a loan once I'm able to find another house for us."

"You can't be serious. Why would you do such a thing? You hardly know me." She went to draw back, already shaking her head as if by doing so she could forget that she'd ever heard him make such a generous offer.

He took another step.

Suddenly she was in his arms, his heart thudding fast and hard against her, his body firm and warm.

"Sara. I think you know why," he murmured.

Then he kissed her.

At first slow, almost tentative as if he thought she'd pull away. But how could she? The idea of his kiss had teased her subconsciousness since the moment she'd met him again. The taste of him on her lips was everything she'd hoped for; the strength surrounding her everything she'd dreamed of.

And suddenly, it felt as if anything was possible.

CHAPTER 10

"Now isn't this cozy," purred a far-too familiar and entirely unexpected voice from behind him.

Darim's gut clenched and edgy anxiety fired every neuron in his brain.

Celeste.

What the devil was his ex-wife doing in Bindarra Creek? She was supposed to be living it up in Paris with her new squeeze.

Ensuring his expression didn't reveal his wariness, he snuffed out his candle and rose to his feet. No way would he give her any advantage including having her look down on him.

"Mum! What are you doing here?" After handing Sara her lit candle, Skye jumped to her feet and hurried around the small grouping of camping chairs to peck her mother on the cheek.

Instead of answering, Celeste fixed her gaze on Sara

who lifted a hand in greeting. There was no smile on Sara's face which remained inscrutable.

For once Darim was appreciative of how effective she was in hiding her feelings. The night was still warm from the heat of the day. Overhead the Milky Way glittered in a canvas of ink and silver while the crescent moon reflected a pale glow above the dark treetops that lined the Akuna River. The evening had been one of the most enjoyable moments of Darim's life. He'd never attended a Carols by Candlelight before and having his precious daughter by his side as well as the woman who now owned his heart had made the entire experience a very special memory. The way he, Sara and Skye had melded together so easily these past couple of weeks as if they had been a unit forever, no longer surprised him; rather he had come to believe it was a blessing and thanked the universe for bringing her into his life again.

But one look at Celeste's narrowed eyes and sneering mouth, warned him fireworks were about to explode.

"Skye is coming home with me," she snapped.

Their daughter glanced from one parent to the other. Darim could see her visibly shrink before his eyes, as her shoulders hunched and she ducked her head. She whispered, "I want to stay with Dad and Sara. You promised I could spend the holidays with him."

"With your father. Not her." Celeste pointed at Sara.

Around them, people began to move away as if keen

to get out of the firing line. Whispers rose competing with the last act of the night which was 'Away in the Manger' sung in a surprisingly beautiful baritone by Warren Myers and accompanied on a keyboard by Pamela Brown.

Senior police sergeant Abby Taylor, who he'd been introduced to earlier that day, leaned forward from where she sat with her family as if ready to intervene if necessary.

Darim met her gaze and gave a little shake of his head. The last thing he wanted was for Celeste's arrival in town becoming the talk of the month. This place was supposed to be a sanctuary for Skye, a place where she could relax and have fun far from the demands of her mother and the life her mother dictated she live. He might have little say in how Celeste insisted she raised their child, but by oath he'd do everything possible to protect his little girl.

"As per our agreement, Skye will remain here." He maintained a level tone of voice but his effort only seemed to spur her on.

She all but spat out, "So you're fine with your daughter spending time with a felon?"

Darim frowned and shot a quick look at Sara who began to stand. "Felon?"

"So your girlfriend didn't tell you about her past convictions for fraud and embezzlement?"

"I can explain ..." Sara started to say.

"Save it!" Celeste waved a hand in the air. "I'm not interested in your petty excuses. It's probably more lies anyway. People like you don't deserve to be listened to; you should be locked away from decent society for good."

"Let's take this discussion out of the public domain, shall we?" He wrapped a hand around Celeste's wrist and tugged. Hard. Anger, doubt and disbelief began a war deep in his brain. He had a hard time processing exactly what was happening in front of him. "Skye. Sara. Grab our gear and head for the car park. We can talk there."

Celeste wrenched out of his grasp and stalked off, saying over her shoulder, "By all means let's hush up your stupidity, Darim. We don't want anyone else realising how much of a fool you are."

Gritting his teeth, he snatched up the esky and plucked a camp chair under his arm then waved the other two in front of him. No one spoke. Feeling as if he was escorting prisoners, he stalked to where they'd left the car.

There were only a few other people in the car park. A young couple piling three sleepy kids into the back seat of their vehicle; and a group of elderly citizens who climbed into a mini-bus obviously waiting for their driver to appear. They only had a few minutes before the concert ended and the lot would be flooded with people heading home.

He stowed their gear away in the back of the Land Rover then turned around and leant on the side of his car. "You'll have to find your own way home, Celeste. Where are you staying?"

"Well." She appeared to be taken aback by his lack of hospitality. "I thought I'd stay with you and Skye. Just like old times." Apparently oblivious to the way she'd acted and her comments of a moment ago, she placed a hand on his shoulder and leaned close.

"That's a definite negative." He pushed her away.

"Have it your way." She tossed back her salon-perfect mane of blonde hair.

Darim rubbed a hand along his jaw and looked to Skye who looked as if she was about to cry. He didn't think he was ready to look at Sara yet. "I take it you've been talking to your mother."

Skye nodded.

"It's okay, Skye." Sara put an arm around the young girl and gave her a brief hug before letting her go. "It's natural that you would let your mum know what you've been doing and who with. No one is angry with you."

"I didn't mean to cause any trouble." Skye's voice shook. A tear dripped down her cheek as she stared at her stone-faced mother.

"You're not the one who's done anything wrong, darling. It's your father. He never should have kept that woman's existence a secret, and certainly not allowed a felon anywhere near you." She shuddered. "God only knows what poisonous ideas she's been drip feeding you."

"I like Sara! She's cool and is going to teach me how to make a llama rug."

"Geeze, Celeste. Stop with all this melodrama!" Darim snapped.

Celeste shook her head. "See, Darim? Already that woman has influenced her."

Head whirling, he battled the growing mistrust his ex-wife had seeded. Sara couldn't be a criminal. He knew her. Knew her inner integrity and bone-deep kindness. He wouldn't and couldn't believe that she would keep such a terrible thing from him. He stepped forward, into Sara's personal space and placed a finger under her chin. "I don't believe a word of what she is saying, Sara. I know Celeste. She likes to make trouble."

But the moment Sara met his eyes, his heart dropped to the bottom of his boots.

There was a deep sadness and shame shining there that couldn't be mistaken.

"She's correct. I was convicted and served time." She spoke flatly as if she was talking about someone else not herself then fell silent. Her mouth had a mulish tilt to it he recognised.

"Sara. Oh, Sara, why didn't you tell me?" He thought about that moment in the solicitor's office when they had met again and how on edge she'd acted. She had obviously been afraid that whatever Ty had been about to tell them would reveal her record. Now Darim began to understand why she was so reticent about her past and why she was so aloof with other people. But whatever she had done, he still couldn't believe that she was a bad person. But why then didn't she say something in her defense? Why just stand there as if she was about to walk away? Was it because she didn't care enough? Maybe she just didn't care about him and Skye as much as he thought and hoped she did.

He stepped back, his hand dropping to his side.

As he did so, her face hardened. That inscrutable mask she wore so well cemented back in place as if the past happy days had never happened.

And something inside him withered.

He could feel his own walls bricking up. "Nothing to say?" he said coldly.

"There isn't anything to say. I did the crime; I did my time."

Eyes almost bugging from their sockets, Skye gasped and placed a hand over her mouth.

Even Celeste was momentarily shocked.

No one was more cut to the core than him as his eyes drilled into Sara's, desperate to slice through her barriers and unmask the truth. Because despite his disillusionment, he suspected there was more that she wasn't telling. But it seemed she didn't trust him enough to divulge the truth or her motives. If there was no trust then there was nothing. He couldn't and wouldn't take a chance on a woman he couldn't trust. Heart and hopes crushed, he turned his back. "Celeste, Skye, get in the car."

"Oh goody. Goodbye Sara. It was … interesting." Celeste smirked and climbed into the Land Rover so fast she probably thought he would change his mind.

Thinking that he probably had lost his mind, Darim ushered his daughter onto the back seat.

"What about Sara, Dad? We can't leave her here," she whispered. Her eyes were wide, cheeks wet with tears, and she was trembling.

He enfolded her hands in his and managed a smile. "It'll be okay, I promise, but its best that she doesn't come home tonight."

"But what about tomorrow? And the next day? And why did Mum have to come here anyway? Why isn't she in France?"

"Good questions which I can't answer yet. Buckle up." He swung back only to find the space where Sara had been standing was empty.

He craned his head in all directions.

But Sara was gone.

WHEN DARIM WOKE the next morning from a fitful sleep the hollowness in his chest reminded him how his future hopes and dreams had disintegrated into ash. He dragged himself from the caravan and after dressing in fresh clothes, found himself outside, feet rooted to the ground and staring at the house. Sara should be inside. She should be sleeping or busy at the stove getting their breakfast. Instead, he knew when he stepped over that threshold he would find his ex-wife in her place.

Given how broken he'd felt last night, he had been unable to stomach any more explanations or another tirade from Celeste. He'd seen her and Skye safely inside and stumbled off to a lonely bunk where he'd tossed and turned; and mourned.

The thought of food made his gut cramp, nevertheless his little girl needed to eat so he crossed to the house where he knocked on the door. First time for everything.

After hearing his ex's snappy response, he entered and without looking towards where the sleeping area he made for the kitchenette. Something easy. Celeste wouldn't eat. She never ate. How she survived had always been a mystery to him. He heated milk and poured it over a couple of Weet-Bix just as Skye walked over.

"Good morning, hon."

"Huh."

He shot her a glance.

Skye's pout reminded him of her mother which made him shudder inside. But his daughter's swollen, red eyes told him she was deeply unhappy.

"I'm sorry everything turned out the way it did," he admitted wondering whether he dared give her a hug and kiss.

She took the bowl off him. "I am, too. I like her, Dad."

"Yeah. Same," was the best he could manage to say.

They both looked around as Celeste wandered into view.

"Is that breakfast?" She gave a mock shudder. "I'll have an Evian water with a slice of lemon and another of lime."

Darim rolled his eyes. "Not gonna happen. It's water or black coffee."

"This is worse than I expected." She sniffed. "And this place. It's hardly what I'd call a house."

"Why are you here?" He held up a hand when she opened her mouth. "Leave off Sara for the moment. What happened with Paris?"

Celeste picked at a loose piece of thread hanging from the negligee she wore. There had been a time, many many years ago when the thought and the sight of her in nightwear would have sent his testosterone raging. These days, he only felt irritation.

"I decided that I wanted to spend Christmas with my baby."

This time it was Skye who rolled her eyes. She grabbed the orange juice from the fridge and stomped out the door with her breakfast.

"What did I say?"

"How about the truth."

"Isn't that funny coming from you." Celeste flopped onto the stool. The same stool that Sara usually perched on while she watched him fry bacon and eggs.

"So I fudged the details a bit about the accommodation. Big deal. Skye is happy here and she's all that matters."

Celeste latched onto his comment eagerly. "Exactly."

He simply raised a brow and leaned back against the cupboard.

"Alright. Paris didn't happen. Our little fling is over.

Are you happy? Antoine had some emergency thing with his wife."

"He's married?"

"Don't be such a prude!" She flapped a hand in the air. "You can't talk. What about your precious Sara?"

"That is different. Leave her out of it."

Celeste stopped smiling and squinted. She really should get stronger contacts or get something done about her eyesight. "When Skye texted me how some woman was living with you, I did a little digging on the internet. The information wasn't hard to find. You've really got it bad, haven't you?"

"You have no idea."

Celeste slid off the stool and coming over, laid a hand on his arm. She cooed, "I forgive you. Why I'm really here is because I want to try again. You and me. It's what Skye would love most of all, to see us together. For us to be a family again. What do you say, Darim? Let's get re-married for our daughter's sake."

CHAPTER 11

eat poured from the brilliant blue sky and simmered from the earth beneath Sara's sneakered feet as she hammered in the last peg holding fast the *'Palms Read & Fortune's Told'* gazebo. Its purple gauzed curtains hung limp in the still air. Everywhere she looked, were smiling faces and happy people. It only served to make her feel more isolated as Lette Park began to swell with Bindarra Creek's inhabitants. Not for the first time did she wonder whether she should have avoided the Christmas Eve Community picnic altogether. But she needed to see him. Whether he wanted to see her was another matter entirely.

After that witch's announcement and not wanting to hang around to face Darim's rejection, Sara had done what she did best – retreated. She needed time alone to think.

More than that she needed time to nurse her wounded heart.

But as the days passed and loneliness ate like poison inside, she finally accepted she had to face her demons. Even if the result was rejection from the man she loved.

"That should do it." Satisfaction oozed from Ms. Edwina Lette's voice from where she perched on a scarlet and flame coloured cushion. Reposing in a wicker picnic basket that had been transformed into a dog carrier sat her new puppy. Boris panted happily and watched with bright brown eyes.

"You could have helped."

"Pwush. I'm under orders from the doc to take it easy."

Sara straightened and after pulling a tissue from the pocket of her red dress, dabbed the sweat prickling her hairline. "Dodge will be happy to know that you're obeying instructions for once," she responded wryly knowing full well the elderly woman only listened to others when it suited her. That meant she had her reasons for hanging around instead of hanging with her cronies who not only formed Bindarra Creek's formidable bush telegraph but were also behind most of the small town's recent transformation into a thriving community. She shot Edwina a suspicious glance then tucked the hammer into her small toolbox. After securing the box, she placed it neatly by her feet. "You want something. That's why you rounded up Dodge to find me and insist I help out today."

An expression flittered across the older woman's face too fast for Sara to interpret as she scrambled from the cushion.

Sara moved over to help.

"It's not what I want – it's what you want, child." Faster than a striking snake, Ms. Lette snatched Sara's hand. But instead of turning it over and mumbling her usual parlour tricks, she clasped it gently in between both of hers and fell silent for several minutes.

Laughter and chatter hummed in the hot air. The Christmas Eve community picnic was gathering speed with every tick of the clock as more and more people arrived in the park. Some headed straight to stake a claim in a patch of grass by setting up their own gazebos or picnic rugs and camping chairs. Others had covered the park's timber tables with food and eskies. More were checking out the booths and stalls, or placing their names with volunteers for sack races, three-legged races, and the egg and spoon races. The mobile rock climb was in the process of being erected while several elves decorated the rotunda for Santa's visit later in the day.

Senior police constable Abby Taylor in her uniform strolled by, her little chihuahua Pinky tucked under one arm. Her husband, captain of the local SES, set down a massive esky beside one of the free barbeques. Several other SES members joined him, along with his and Abby's two red-headed sons Drew and Eddie. As soon as the boys set down their burdens of foil covered trays, they quickly sidled away joining a group of smiling teenagers. Kids rushed everywhere, squealing with joy on the swings. The crowd of children and their parents over by the brand-new splash pool was growing larger by the second. The pool which was still barricaded by police tape had yet to be opened by the mayor. Judging by the kids' avid almost feral excitement, that had better happen soon or there'd be a stampede into the water. If the heat continued throughout the day, more than kids would be paddling in that pool by day's end.

"You're too wary, Sara. It's time to move on from the past."

A lump clogged Sara's throat. She had to swallow hard in order to speak. "You don't know ..." She stopped, couldn't continue, couldn't reveal the full extent of her shame to a woman who had shown her nothing but kindness.

"No, I don't. But I know my grandson and he considers you to be a woman of integrity. One of his closest friends, actually. And I've come to know you myself since you've been here, and I like what I know. You're not alone, Sara. Dodge, Warren, Tessa, Lou and all the kids as well as me – well, you're part of our family now. Whether you like it or not." The last was flung out like a challenge but with an accompanying warm smile.

Eyes stinging, Sara remained mute, her tongue feeling glued to her mouth.

She wasn't alone.

They wanted her to be part of their family.

Edwina wasn't done with her yet. She gave the hand she held a gentle tug. "You could have more if you can find the courage. That hottie Darim and his lovely daughter could be yours too. All you have to do is give it your best shot. You have nothing to lose but your pride. And everything to gain." She winked. "I just gave the same advice to that archaeologist fellow, Ernest Callen. Never saw a man move so fast in my life. He almost fell over his own feet in his haste to find Fatima."

Sara fastened on the side topic as if it was a life jacket and she was drowning. "Fatima? You mean Natalie's friend and Darim's sister …?"

"Looks like it." Triumph rang clear in Edwina's smug tones. "Well? Hadn't you better get moving yourself?"

"I was going to but … I'm ashamed. What if …?" blurted Sara.

"Oh, child. We've all done things we'd prefer to forget, or wish had never happened. If he can't look past that then it wasn't meant to be. Now, come here." Edwina dropped the hand she held and folded Sara in her arms.

As she returned the hug, Sara couldn't help noticing how small and thin the old lady was – not surprising after she'd nearly died a few months ago when a desperate man kidnapped her and held her hostage. However, she'd been found in time. Although her physical recovery had a long way to go before she was back to her former healthy self, nothing dampened Edwina Lette's spirits.

Heart feeling as if it would burst, Sara drew away.

"Be honest. With what you did and why. Then be honest with how you feel. Now, I had better get cracking. Where did I put my crystal ball?" Edwina began to rummage in a plastic tub.

Boris uttered a sharp yap, as if unhappy to be ignored.

"There's a good boy." Eyes blurred, Sara bent down and rubbed his cute floppy ears.

Edwina scooped up a pile of cushions and chucked them inside the tent, before following suit with the tub.

Picking up the basket, Sara carried Boris inside and laid him carefully next to the small boho table while the other woman organized her tarot cards and crystal ball.

"Anything else you need help with?" She sniffed and blew her nose with the tissue before balling it up and chucking into a rubbish bin.

"Nope. All good. See you later. Don't forget to join us for lunch. I won't ask any questions." Ms. Lette settled onto a cushion and plopped Boris onto her lap. "And in my opinion, if he's got any sense there is no way he could resist you and your red dress."

A second later, Sara found herself standing outside the purple tent. Her head whirled while her pulse thrummed hard and fast through her body energising every single atom she possessed.

Darim.

No more excuses. She had to find him.

Had to tell him.

Had to hope that her silly mistletoe wish would come true.

And then she would accept whatever outcome the universe chose to bestow.

Feeling as if she was going to her execution, Sara rounded the dunking stand and came face to face with Darim. He was alone.

The grim expression on a face filled with purpose sent a rush of burning heat that dissolved her insides to mush.

"I've been looking everywhere for you."

Shifting her hold on her small toolbox, she flittered her gaze around at the milling crowd. Laughter. Squeals. Excited conversations. Couples holding hands. Families bunched together smiling. They all flowed like so much white noise past her ears.

Desperate to prolong the moment of her confession, she asked, "Where's Skye?"

"She's with her cousins and keeping an eye on the llamas."

"And Celeste? Is she … has she gone?"

"Yes. Thank heavens. I paid for an uber to drive her out of town the morning after the concert."

Sara tilted her head, mulling over his words. "She didn't take Skye then?"

"No. She didn't want to go anyway. We need to talk." He caught hold of her hand and tugged her around the back of the stalls. They crossed the freshly mown grass to stand beneath a shady jacaranda tree. "These past days have been hell. It's not a situation I ever wanted to find myself in again after my marriage ended. But there you have it. Where have you been? I contacted everyone I could think of, but no one has heard from you in days."

"I've been re-evaluating my life choices." Sara's heart all but exploded out of her chest so fast was it pounding.

"Were you hiding out at Fig Tree Lodge with Dodge and his family?"

"No. I camped in Akuna National Park."

"You look thinner. Have you been eating properly?"

Did he really care? She shrugged, trying to beat down the flickering hope that refused to die. "With the fire ban, I couldn't cook so I've been living off tins of baked beans and fruit."

"Geeze, Sara. I've been so worried." He dragged his free hand through his short hair, causing the ends to stand up. But his other thumb caressed the back of her knuckles. "That solicitor doesn't know you've gone AWOL from the property. I've also contacted my Sydney lawyer and set in motion my withdrawal from the bequest."

"You shouldn't have done that." She slipped her hand from his hold and placed the toolbox on the ground. By doing so, she managed to create a little more space between them. She couldn't catch hold of her thoughts standing so close to him. Not when with every fibre of her being, she hungered to be in his arms.

Even if it was for only one last time.

Judging by his swift frown, Darim was fully alive as to the reason behind her movement. His gaze hooked hers and held. "I'm a man of my word, Sara."

"I know. But I'm not worthy of your generosity."

"How about you let me be the judge of that. I'm in love with you."

Her fingers twitched. A tension headache began to stab behind her eyes as she fought the urge to run from him, from her past. "I can't believe you still feel that way – not after what your wife told you."

"Ex. She is in my past. I thought you were my future." He stepped forward and held her upper arms gently. "You still are my future, unless you convince me that you don't want me in your life."

"If you really knew what I'm capable of you would walk away and never look back."

"Why don't you tell me what happened?"

She licked her cracked lips. This was it. The moment of truth. She couldn't hold back any longer. Besides, she was relieved to finally tell someone the whole story, and glad that it was him.

"All right then. Here goes. I was a cop. I'd been assigned a temporary position helping bag and record a ton of evidence from a recent drug raid. Along with drugs, taped interviews and other documentation there was also the cash seized as part of the alleged money laundering operation. According to one of the investigation officer's records, there was supposed to be one point four million dollars in fifty-dollar notes. I don't know what came over me." Clenching her fists, she hung her head. "But when I saw that money, I couldn't stop myself from thinking that just a portion could be the salvation I'd been praying for. My parents needed twenty-four seven nursing care. They were both uneducated having been brought up in an orphanage – that's where they met. They barely scrapped a living as times were tough in South Korea under the military regime at that time. In 1983 they came to Australia as refugees and were granted asylum. Then they had me – their miracle baby. The child expected to raise them out of poverty and look after them in their old age. I did everything I was expected to do; studied hard, worked even harder at my job as a police officer, obtained a mortgage to buy a small unit for them to live in. But their health declined rapidly, and all my spare money was going into paying their bills. The doctor said they required more help than I could afford to keep them living in their own home. They were terrified of being separated and going into a nursing home. I didn't know what to do to help."

As the memories poured back, so did the shame and failure. Shaking in her skin, her shoulders sagged as she covered her face with her hands.

"Not a good situation for anyone to find themselves in." A kiss landed on the top of her head.

It took all her willpower not to lean forward and rest against his strong chest. She had to keep going;

had to tell him the entire truth. If he washed his hands of her, at least she had owned up to her past mistakes. And there would be no more secrets.

"The other two officers working with me where at the other side of the room. No one was watching and where I stood was a blind spot for the security cameras. I counted the money. I thought one hundred thousand would buy me some time. The trial wasn't for another eight months. Plenty of time for me to get a second mortgage over the unit and replace the cash. But the thing is ..." she paused and lifted her hands from her face.

The noise of the community picnic ebbed as if the world was poised for her to continue. A flock of black cockatoos passed overhead, squawking as they flew, making her jump. She usually wasn't this easily startled. Just went to show exactly how much this conversation meant to her. It could signal the end of her most secret desire – to belong.

Through her silent tears she met his impassive gaze. "Only fifty thousand dollars was there; beneath the first few real notes in each bundle was a pile of paper cut to the same size. Someone had beat me to it. I think it was then that it really hit me that if I took the money, I'd be a criminal. No better than the scum I'd dedicated my career to taking down. I changed my mind but I wasn't certain who to trust about the missing money. I picked up four bundles and stuffed them down my shirt thinking that I would take them to Dodge, and we'd work out how to proceed from there. Stupid.

Stupid. I was panicking and couldn't think straight. Later, Dodge saw me stashing them into my handbag in the locker room but before I could talk to him the next thing I knew I was being hauled in front of Internal Affairs."

"Then you were innocent."

She shook her head. "Not really. I was going to steal that money."

"But you didn't."

"No one believed me that I changed my mind. I was caught with the evidence on my person. Afterwards, Dodge got his uncle who is an awesome barrister onto my case; pro bono which was good of him. One day I'll pay them back. His team made so much stink over the charges against me and the circumstances, a royal commission into the whole mess was instigated. Because I cooperated with the investigation and fully admitted my intentions, plus they took into account my previous good record as a cop, in the end I was given a suspended sentence. It took a good two years however for all this to play out. In the meantime, I was in jail. My parents died alone. I never got to say goodbye or how sorry I was for leaving them the way I did and how ashamed I was that I had disappointed them."

"That's one hell of an ordeal."

"Don't you mean story? Apart from Dodge, not one other of my colleagues believed me. Even though I ended up being vindicated and the real culprits discovered and charged, most cops will never trust me again." Her voice cracked on the last word.

He nudged her chin with his hand. "I trust you, Sara. I've come to know the real you over the past couple of weeks. We all make bad choices."

"Not as bad as me."

"Hey. I'm no lily-white hero who's always done the right thing at the right time. I've sent men and women into a battle I had doubts we could win. What does that make me?"

"That's different. That's war and you were only doing your duty."

"Still doesn't make it any easier to forget or stop blaming yourself. I remember every soldier who died or was injured under my command. What I'm trying to say is that no one is perfect or infallible. We all have pasts we wish we could forget. But I believe if we learn from our mistakes that ends up making us better people in the end. And that's all anyone can hope for. To be a better person. I can forgive you, Sara. The question is – can you forgive yourself? Can you make a choice to move on and take another chance on life? With me?" He slid his hands down her arms and took hold of both her hands.

His touch was firm but careful, as if giving her the option of slipping away. "I want you to be part of my family, Sara. You, Skye and me. Maybe there could even be a rugrat or two in our future, too. Whatever happens, this is our opportunity to start again. Our second chance."

Eyes burning with a storm of emotions threatening to pull her down into the darkness she'd thought at one time, she'd never escape, Sara hesitated. She'd been granted her mistletoe wish – to have a family of her own again. To be loved. To be considered worthy of trust and respect. Could she forgive herself for failing her parents when they needed her most? Should she accept this gift? If she did, there would probably be times in the future when she would doubt herself and grieve over what she couldn't change.

But that was life – love, grief, joy and sadness, it was all part of connecting with others, of being part of the world. Of living.

She was ready to make her decision.

CHAPTER 12

Who would have thought that assisting a stranger on a lonely country road would have led her here to this moment – this time – and this amazing man. And yet here she was; not only did she have Darim and his daughter in her life but she was surrounded by people who more than accepted her; they liked her. A realisation that humbled her to her toes. Never again would she take her family or friends for granted. She'd been blessed with another chance that she had no intentions of messing up.

Not this time round.

Sara took a moment to send a heartfelt thanks to the universe then shuffled forward in the pet parade queue; one of the highlights of the community's Christmas Eve picnic. She grinned as a cheer erupted from Darim who stood on the sidelines taking pics of Skye leading Sara's beautiful brown cria, Cher, while she led Sonny, a slightly older male cria. Both llamas were liberally decorated with red tinsel and sported antlers where tiny bells tinkled with each halting step they took. Cher even wore a red and white Santa top. They weren't that keen on the noise swelling from the crowd like ocean waves pounding a shoreline and kept throwing their heads up. Normally, placid animals they were becoming a trifle jittery. She made a mental note to spend a lot of time grooming and fussing over them when she had them back home.

Home.

Hard to believe she had finally admitted that word to herself.

She had a home and two people in her life who meant the world to her.

"That's my girls!" Darim pumped the air with his fist. Pride glowed in his brown eyes along with a sparking heat that fanned her senses into flames.

"By the way, how did you get the llamas here?" she asked as she came closer.

"I contacted Grady Ferguson and he leant me the horse float again. I've got to return it tomorrow however as he needs it."

"Thanks. I'm glad we were able to make good on the promise I made Skye."

A teenage boy strolled by; one hand in his pocket the other leading a well-behaved dog in a yellow shirt which had the word *'lifeguard'* printed in red, and a surf life-saving cap tied with string around his neck. Noah Davidson and his dog, Chip. Somehow even with her tongue hanging out the dog managed a huge yawn. But she was one of the few animals who were behaving themselves; several began to revolt against trotting about in the heat and wearing silly outfits. A donkey brayed then a rabbit hopped past followed by a crying child. A dog in a green jacket and with reindeer antlers half slipping off his head raced past being chased by a Christmas elf. Then Sonny dug his back hooves into the grass and spat narrowly missing one of the judges.

Sara broke into laughter along with just about everyone else. The explosion of noise and chaos spooked Cher. She bolted into a trot with Skye hanging onto her bridle, begging him to stop in between her giggles. She finally brought the young llama to a halt and dragged her back towards where Sara and Darim watched with broad grins on their faces.

"We're the only ones with a weird entry in the pet parade." Darim chuckled. "I reckon next year we'll have to come up with something to top our llamas. I'm thinking you and me in a llama costume. Skye can be our handler."

Next year. He was already talking about their future. Bless the man. She ran a soothing hand over Cher who quietened even more than checked Sonny but he seemed to be happy enough standing patiently by her side. She laid a hand on Darim's arm which he instantly captured and raising it to his mouth, kissed her knuckles. Her cheeks heated as she saw the sidelong looks and elbowing that went on by Natalie and Troy Davidson who were standing close by.

But it was about time that she learnt to ignore the

good-natured nosiness of this small town. So raising herself on tiptoe, she pressed her lips against his.

In an instant his arms were iron bands around her back, drawing her hard and urgent against his chest. His returning kiss thrilled her to the soles of her feet and the surrounding power of his muscles made her feel as if he would always protect her.

"About time. I thought you two would never kiss," came Skye's amused voice.

Breathless and wanting more, Sara emerged from Darim's embrace. They smiled at each other as Sonny leaned forward and stuck his head in between them as if wanting to be included.

"And no, you can't get a room. Not yet anyway. I'm starved. Is it lunch time already?" Grinning, Skye slung an arm around both of them, jerking the reins. Cher jolted Sonny sideways, so he snorted then sent a stream of water in her direction.

Darim huffed out an explosive breath and quickly dodged the spit. "What the devil do you know about getting a room?" He took the reins off his daughter.

"Dad. Please. I'm twelve not two." Skye gave a dramatic eye roll, "Living with Mum you grow up fast."

His lips thinned and a dangerous glint appeared in his eyes.

But before he could say anything, his daughter planted a kiss on his cheek. "It's okay. I'm still your little girl."

"You'll always be my little girl," Darim said gruffly and, one armed, pulled her to him.

"And don't you forget it." Skye turned to Sara and hugged her, too. "I'm so happy you're going to be my step-mum."

"Woah, kiddo. What are you doing? You're stealing my thunder."

"Dad, if Sara waited for you to get your act into gear, she'll be a hundred. And I wouldn't mind a little brother or sister. Now, come on, let's put Cher and Sonny somewhere safe and get some food." She linked arms with them as they strolled away from the pet parade.

A little brother or sister. Whether that would happen, Sara, had no idea. It would be wonderful if it did, however if it didn't then she was more than satisfied with the family she already had.

From the rotunda came the squeal of the microphone then the band burst into an energetic rendering of *'All I want for Christmas.'*

"We've been invited to join the Myer family and their friends for lunch." Sara gazed around the park as they secured the llamas beneath a tree and placed a full bucket of water nearby. "There they are; under the Morton Bay fig tree and with the red and green gazebo."

"I see them." Darim gave a soundless whistle. "That's quite a crowd. Sure there'll be anything left for us?" But his voice was teasing.

Skye groaned. "There had better be, or I'm having barbequed llama!"

Darim insisted they wait however until after the

mayor opened the new children's splash pool before heading over and joining the Lette and Myers' party. They waved to his sister who was sitting on a park bench with Ernest sharing what looked like a glass of bubbly. As soon as she'd been handed a sausage sandwich, Skye was urged by Kaylee to join in a volleyball game. Sara settled onto the picnic rug with Darim, although she could barely swallow her lunch. The kids weren't the only ones giddy with excitement.

"If you'd like, we could tell everyone our news?" Darim whispered as he snuggled close despite the heat.

Sara nudged his ear with the tip of her nose then smiled. "I don't remember you asking."

"Then how about you give me time to organise the asking in style. I want it to be special, sweetheart."

"So do I. Anyway, I know your motive. You don't want to give up the bequest." She giggled when he poked her ribs.

He laughed. "You've caught me."

"Anything you want to tell us, child?"

Sara looked up to meet Ms. Lette's twinkling eyes and shook her head. Not that she fooled that old lady who simply laid a finger against the side of her nose and winked.

Tessa opened her mouth probably to interrogate her when there came the familiar 'eh-aw' of the fire engine. Children screamed and ran like one massive cloud of locusts. Parents and grandparents and older teenagers moved far more languidly.

"Let's go watch." Darim pulled her to her feet as

Skye raced over, her face flushed pink. "Here. Drink." He offered a full bottle of water.

"I wouldn't mind having a go at the dunking game later," Sara said, adjusting her hat over her hair.

"Me too." Skye chugged down half the bottle then added in a gruff voice, "What time is Santa coming?" She might act older than her years most of the time, but her gentle query was a subtle reminder that she was not quite a teenager yet.

"That's him now, on the fire truck." A tiny trickle of perspiration formed above Sara's upper lip. She hoped she'd done the right thing and that Skye wouldn't be too embarrassed or feel awkward.

"What is it?"

She met Darim's frowning gaze. He'd picked up on her change in mood in an instant and yet they'd only known each other for … what … three weeks? It made her wonder if they would end up being one of those couples who in their old age knew each other so well, they could have been telepathic. She leaned forward and whispered in his ear.

"What's going on?" Skye asked.

"You'll see." Darim linked his fingers with Sara's and they strolled over to the rotunda. They were in time to see Paddy Cullen dressed as Santa Clause – well, an Australian Santa. Although his outfit was the customary red and white, his sleeves were rolled up above his elbows and he wore red shorts that revealed his knobby knees, thongs adorned his feet and he had dark sunnies covering his eyes.

The fire brigade captain, Kel Jones carried the Santa sack as Paddy climbed down from the back of the fire truck and crossed to the rotunda where a throne had been installed. There were any number of Santa helpers, most dressed as elves, standing beside several other sacks. A hush fell over the crowd.

Paddy aka Santa settled into his chair with a groan and immediately asked for a cold beer. Someone handed him a bottle of water and a list and a microphone.

"What's going on?" asked Skye.

"No idea. But I think Sara does." Darim gave Sara a teasing smile but she placed her finger to her lips and shook her head.

"Who's been naughty and who's been nice?" Roared Paddy over the microphone.

Hands shot up from the kids and several of the adults, too.

Then he began to read out names. As each child's name was called, one of the helpers would trot through the crowd, single out the named kid and tow them to the rotunda where a present was placed in their hands. A gold wrapped parcel for the girls and silver for the boys; each coming from a different sack depending on the age of the child.

"This is perfect. Who organised this?" Darim whispered to Sara.

"Mostly the CWA ladies are behind it courtesy of some generous businesses. This way every kid in town will get a present regardless of how tough the year may have been for their parents."

"It's brilliant."

"Skye Cooper," bellowed Paddy from the stage.

"That's me. That's my name." Skye gaped at her father.

"Go on then. Off you go." He shooed her into the hands of a waiting elf then turned to Sara. "Why were you worried about this?"

"I wasn't certain how she would take her inclusion given she's only here for the holidays. And especially since I was the one who ensured she was on the list. She barely knows me."

He very tenderly pressed his lips to hers. "Sara. You can tell from her reaction it was a fabulous idea. There is nothing to be worried about. You. Me. Skye. We're going to do just fine. We're a family now."

A family.

Her mistletoe wish had come true.

Darim pulled her back against his chest and wrapped his arms around her waist. Together they watched as Skye with a huge grin on her face skipped towards them, waving a gold wrapped present in the air and calling out, "I can't believe you didn't get me a llama!"

From the Author

Thank you so much for taking the time to read my Bindarra Creek Christmas romance ***The Mistletoe Wish.*** For this series, I decided that it was time for Sara to reveal her story and find her happy-ever-after. She helped foil a stalker in Bindarra Creek Makeover and was one of the many who were unrelenting in their search when one of their own was kidnapped in Amulet of Death. I hope dear reader that you enjoyed her journey.

If you would like to read more sweet small-town romances, my other Bindarra Creek books (***Bindarra Creek Makeover, Love's Sweet Challenge, Take me Home*** and ***Amulet of Death***) are available for sale as ebooks and also paperbacks.

ABOUT THE MULTI-AUTHOR BINDARRA CREEK SERIES

Welcome to Bindarra Creek, a struggling country town where people work hard and love deeply. Set in the picturesque tablelands of New England, Australia, Bindarra Creek is a fictional, rural community full of romance, intrigue, adventure, drama and suspense. The other books in this world are:

Bindarra Creek Romance
Bindarra Creek Makeover - S. E. Gilchrist
Shadows of the Heart - Lee Christine
Second Chance Love - Susanne Bellamy
The CEO Mechanic - Sandie James (not available)
Reach for the Stars - Kerrie Paterson
Home to Bindarra Creek - Juanita Kees
Stolen Sanctuary - Stacey Nash
Tempting Fate - Erin Moira O'Hara
One More Day - Linda Charles
The Vine - Lauren K. McKellar

The Ghost of His Past - Simone Angela
Joanie's Dilemma - Marianne Theresa
Buckley's Chance - Noelle Clark

Bindarra Creek Short & Sweet

What's in a Kiss – Linda Charles
My Forever Valentine – Sandie James (not available)
Pearls and Green Beer – Susanne Bellamy
Full Circle – Annie Seaton
Date with Destiny – Erin Moira O'Hara
A Letter From the Queen – Lee Christine
Love's Sweet Challenge – Suzanne Gilchrist (aka S E Gilchrist)
The Widow Maker – Lauren K. McKellar
Out of the Blue – Noelle Clark

Bindarra Creek A Town Reborn

Take Me Home – Suzanne Gilchrist (aka S E Gilchrist)
In the Heat of the Night – Susanne Bellamy
No Looking Back - Linda Charles
Worth the Wait – Annie Seaton
With Every Breath – Lauren K. McKellar
Stealing Her Heart – Simone Angela
A Twist of Fate – Erin Moira O'Hara
Promise Me Forever – Juanita Kees

Bindarra Creek Mystery Romance

Amulet of Death – Suzanne Gilchrist (aka S E Gilchrist)
Beyond the Gate – Rhonda Forrest
Protecting their Destiny – Erin Moira O'Hara
Only She Knew – Linda Charles
Secrets of River Cottage – Annie Seaton
Forgotten Secrets – Susanne Bellamy
A Perfect Danger – Phillipa Nefri Clark

Bindarra Creek Christmas Romance

The Mistletoe Wish - Suzanne Gilchrist (aka S E Gilchrist)
A Clever Christmas - Annie Seaton
Mistletoe Magic - Erin Moira O'Hara
Christmas Jinx - Susanne Bellamy
Tangled by Tinsel - Phillipa Nefri Clark
The Grinch of Bindarra Creek - Lindsay Douglas
Mistletoe and Blue Jeans - Linda Charles
Christmas at Forrest Glen - Rhonda Forrest
A Cowboy for Christmas - Lauren K McKellar

Full details on buy links for all books in Bindarra Creek world can be found on the website: www.bindarracreekromance.com

EXCERPTS

For your reading pleasure, here is an excerpt from my book, Amulet of Death (Bindarra Creek Mystery Romance):

S*ydney Barracks,*
16th October, 1914.
Dear family,

Many happy returns, mother and may God grant you many more. Alfred and I are going strong. Do try and not worry. Tell father not to hire Roaming Jack for shearing this year. Too many bloodied sheep the last time he was on our farm. There is plenty of tucker although it is always the same. Nothing like your home cooking mother which I miss dearly. Like our tucker our days are the same. We rise at dawn, march from the barracks to Rosebery, no idea why and back again. There is bayonet practise and we exercise constantly. I suppose we must be in tiptop shape so we can fight the Jerries. Rumour is our squad will leave our shores in the next week or two. It will be bonzers to be on our way. I have taken up learning French, it may prove useful. I am sure we will be home by Christmas.

With love to all, I remain your affect. son and brother, Mitchell.

Exultation sizzled like an electric current through the man's veins as he stepped off the lowest tread of the rickety stairs and into the gloomy cellar. The old timber creaked underfoot, a thunderbolt of noise in the heavy silence. He paused, his breathing pulsing loud in his ears as he sucked in the stink of mould from years of neglect and damp. His excitement heightened, twisting hard in the pit of his gut and his palms tingled. All those years of study and chasing down every clue no matter how small had led him right to this moment, this place. Finally, he was close to achieving his life-long obsession.

He groped along the grimy wall, unable to find another light switch. Slipping his mobile out from his pants' pocket, he flicked on the torch app, then frowned. Layers of cobwebs clung to the ceiling. Mice droppings mounded in the corners. There were no prints in the thick dust underfoot.

No one had entered the cellar in years.

Not that he intended to give up and turn tail now.

Everything he'd earned in life had been done the hard way which, in turn, had honed his ruthless nature into a brutal and unrelenting weapon. His prize was close – he knew it, and all he had to do was find the clue that would reveal the next link.

He paced further away from the only other light source, a single bulb positioned above the steep stairs, and pushed aside a curtain of sticky, filmy, web. Just as well cramped, dark places didn't bother him. That particular fear had been well and truly conquered years ago – a time in his life that had essentially gone down to the wire – either deal with it or be broken. He had too much innate stubbornness for that to ever happen. A cockroach skittered across the floor and disappeared beneath a broken sideboard. There were a couple of ancient beer barrels stacked against one wall. Three rickety shelving units stood crammed together, blocking any further passage to the right. He had hoped for at least an old tin trunk or a pile of bric-a-brac to examine.

Nothing. His elation faded. But there were still the old woman's private rooms to search. He'd turn the place inside out if he had to. All he needed was time alone.

A warm puff of air wafted over the back of his bare neck – a sudden odd intrusion in the coldness of the silent cellar. It felt like - *like a breath!*

Like someone was behind him.

His heart slammed against his ribs in a sudden

gallop as panic flooded his mind. He stiffened. Whirling thoughts crashed in frantic union with his pounding heart. How could he explain what he was doing prowling about in the cellar? But wait – no one was home. He'd made certain they had all left before he began his search. Then who the dickens stood behind him in weighted silence?

The chill in the cellar increased sending goose-bumps brushing over his skin in a flurry of icy strokes. He shivered as the freezing air sank into his bones. Should he attempt to explain? Or wait for the other to speak first? To his left, there was a flick of a tail as a mouse melted into the darkness as if desperate to escape impending danger. His hand tightened around his mobile. But…

A shadow rippled over the wall – *too late*.

A rush of air behind him – *too late*.

Agony splintered across his skull as lethal as a rock-slide. His vision dimmed to blackness and he crashed to the floor.

AND HERE IS **another excerpt from my book, Take Me Home (Bindarra Creek A Town Reborn:**

THE ICY WINTER night closed in around the paddy wagon, the instant Senior Constable Abigail Taylor killed the engine. Shivering as the heater died and the gusty wind rocked the car on its axles, she pulled her navy-blue beanie over her blonde hair then glanced across at Senior Sergeant Riley Morgan.

"Looks like we have company." Abby nodded to where three figures could be seen, shoulders hunched in their winter coats, hands deep in their pockets, as they stamped their feet on the front porch of Bindarra Creek Police Station.

The security lighting did little to discern their features, hidden beneath hoods pulled low over their faces. An adult and a couple of kids, thought Abby, as she took a sharp visual inventory. The kids kept their backs to the adult, standing a good three metres away as if to emphasise they didn't belong as a unit. Possibly an irate home-owner who had caught the kids in the act of desecrating his fence with graffiti - all in the name of art - or boredom.

More paperwork. More soothing of ruffled feathers. More kids to place on 'clean-up' duty. She bit back her sigh, her hopes of catching the bistro at the Riverside Pub before it closed, disappearing like Halley's Comet over the horizon.

Riley rubbed a hand over his stubbly jaw and mumbled past a wide yawn, "I'll see to it."

Smiling, Abby released her seat belt and slipped the keys from the ignition. "Nope. Leave it to me, boss. You've got a full night ahead of you with that baby of yours."

"Teething!" He groaned. "Never thought baby teeth could cause so much pain."

Ignoring the savage momentary twist of jealousy that gripped her, Abby managed a grin. "For you or the kid?"

"All of us." Meeting her gaze, Riley grimaced. "I'm on night duty tonight while Sam gets some sleep."

"All the more reason for me to deal with whoever is on our front doorstep."

"Thanks. I'll give you a hand, writing up tonight's incident in the morning."

"Sounds like a plan." Eager to avoid any more talk about children, Abby grabbed her thick police-issue jacket from the back of the seat while Riley climbed out the other side of the wagon.

With a brief wave, she pushed open the car door then leaned heavily against it as the wind slammed it back toward her body. "Ouch. I'll be so glad to get out of this weather."

"You okay?" Riley placed his hand on the bonnet.

"Yeah, all good. Thanks. See you bright and early." She pushed her arms into the sleeves of her jacket while Riley sprinted towards the highway patrol car and climbed inside.

A few moments later, his car's taillights disappeared down the road – heading for home. Heading for a hot dinner that was no doubt waiting for him. But definitely heading home to his family.

Family. Something Abby no longer had in her life.

Burying her brief flash of sadness, she turned to the small group waiting for her. With her hands resting lightly on her gel duty belt, she strode the short distance through a buffeting wind so cold it made her eyes water and her nose numb. She lifted her gaze briefly to the dark sky where clouds scudded across the scattering of stars. Too high to portend any rain, unfortunately. The region could do with a good downfall. But an early morning frost could well be on the cards. In other words, a very chilly night.

Flexing her stiff fingers, she stopped on the top step, her heart doing a crazy skip as she recognised the adult. "Elizabeth! What are you doing here?"

"At the moment, trying to keep warm." Elizabeth shuddered. "That wind is so cold."

"Tell me about it. I've just spent the past hour walking around the cemetery searching for non-existent burglars." Abby switched her stare to the two kids, both boys. The taller, was about thirteen or fourteen with a surly, belligerent twist to his mouth, and the other judging by his similar features, was his younger brother. Dark red hair that needed cutting, straggled about their pale, lightly freckled faces. "Who's this?"

"Kids who need your help. I've never forgotten your adoption application, Abby."

"Shame it was never approved." Attempting to act unconcerned, she took another inventory over the scene. Her hands clenched, bitter disappointment scorching her throat and she had to swallow hard over the sudden constriction. She'd thought she'd dealt with it – moved on. Apparently, the past still had the power to cut her to the bone.

"What can I do for you?" She straightened her shoulders as she brushed past the other woman, intending to unlock the door.

"Oh, we're not here on police business." Elizabeth gave a little laugh. It sounded forced.

Eyes narrowed, Abby swung around to face her. "Then why? I haven't heard from you in over four years."

The older woman shuffled her feet. "Can't we go somewhere warmer to talk? Where do you live?"

Abby's stomach grumbled, and she admitted, "I could do with some food. Have you eaten?"

"Yes. We stopped for dinner in Tamworth so we're fine. I'm parked across the road. How about I drive you home? I'd prefer if we were somewhere private and not inside a police station."

Abby recalled her nearly bare pantry and bit back a sigh. She'd have to make do with whatever was left in the cupboard – which was probably very little. For Elizabeth to appear out of the blue, whatever had happened had to be serious. Despite herself, Abby's pulse picked up and tension cramped her belly. "Thanks, but I'm on call and need to take the paddy wagon."

"Then we'll follow you." Elizabeth smiled.

Abby knew that serene look. It masked an iron will. Elizabeth wouldn't explain until she was good and ready. Bowing to the inevitable, she muttered, "Let's go then." She waited while Elizabeth shepherded the two boys across the road and into a white Holden sedan, not moving towards her own vehicle until she heard the other car's engine start.

A few minutes later, Abby drove along Mount Ingalls Road heading to the western section of town. She crossed over Gillies Bridge, and checked the rear vision mirror, noting the following headlights. Her mind teemed with questions while she battled not to acknowledge that stupid and forlorn hope that had refused to die.

Why was Elizabeth here? Was there a chance her adoption application's rejection had been overturned? But if so, why now? After all these years?

And what did those boys have to do with anything?

There were no street lights out here. The road was tarred, single lane and wide with the houses on both sides sitting on either one or several acres of land. Many had large sheds and out-buildings, but few lights shone between curtains drawn tight to shut out the wintry night.

She slowed as she neared the bend, flicked her indicator on to the left then turned off onto a narrow dirt road that led over a cattle grid.

A single light glowed on her verandah and pooled over the front of the house, proving the timer she'd had installed recently had been a good investment. Her car bumped down the driveway, before she pulled up near the steps. After turning off the engine, she exited, smiling as she caught the excited yaps of her tiny dog, Pinky, coming from inside.

Home.

No one rushed to greet her. No lights flicked on to welcome her. Only her dog waited.

For buy links for these books and others, please visit the website www.segilchrist.com

ACKNOWLEDGMENTS

As always a huge thanks to my critique partner, Erin Moira O'Hara, who not only casts her eagle eyes over my manuscripts but who is also a wonderful friend.

I also wish to thank Cindy Pearson for her proofreading skills, and Patti Roberts for my lovely cover.

In the spirit of reconciliation, I acknowledge Aboriginal and Torres Strait Islander peoples as the First Australians and Traditional Custodians of the lands where I live, learn and work. I pay my respects to Elders past, present and emerging, and thank them for their ongoing custodianship of and care for the country I live and write on.

ABOUT SUZANNE GILCHRIST

(AKA S.E. GILCHRIST)

S. E. Gilchrist can't remember a time when she didn't have a book in her hand. Now she dreams up stories where her favourite words are … 'what if' and 'where'? Writing as both S. E. Gilchrist and Suzanne Gilchrist, she loves combining romance with adventure and suspense across many different genres including science fiction/space opera, apocalyptic, and contemporary small towns.

S. E. takes a keen interest in the environment, anything to do with space, and loves walking her two dogs and spending time with her family. Of course, there is nothing better than catching up with friends over a hot cuppa. She co-runs the Hunter Romance Writers group and is the organiser behind the multi-author writing ventures: the best-selling Bindarra Creek Romance series, the Deadly Forces series, and the Mindalby Outback Romance series.

Recently she moved interstate from the lovely Hunter Valley to sunny, southeast Queensland. Now her home is within distance of the city with parklands, the Hinterland and Moreton Bay all on her doorstep.

For more information, visit her www.segilchrist.com